THE CHILDREN OF KUMBHALGARH

and other stories

by

Valerie Thornhill

Highgate Publications (Beverley) Limited
1998

for John, who waited during an elephantine pregnancy

Acknowledgements

John Markham of Highgate Publications for his patience and encouragement; Barry Sage and Barry Ireland of BA Print for pulling out all the stops to have the book ready on time; Stephen Wilton-Ely for excellent proof-reading and advice; Robert Cockcroft for his sensitive and inventive cover design; Susan Cockcroft, without whose positive criticism and unequivocal belief, these stories would never have been published.

British Library Cataloguing in Publication Data.
A catalogue record for this book is available from the British Library.

ISBN 1 902645 01 4

Published by

Highgate of Beverley

Highgate Publications (Beverley) Limited
24 Wylies Road, Beverley, HU17 7AP
Telephone (01482) 866826

Produced by

4 Newbegin, Lairgate, Beverley, HU17 8EG
Telephone (01482) 886017

Cover design by Robert Cockcroft, who invites you to discover which story is not illustrated.

Contents

❦

for Sandra and Lynn, Rummana and Stan

❧

THE CHILDREN OF KUMBHALGARH

'There's someone in my room!' Stifled yawns of 'not her again!' spread through the small group breakfasting in the tourist Lodge that chilly February morning. ' I was just opening the door and heard someone moving around.' Alicia Thwaite's plump hands were trembling. Her husband took the keys; they watched him make his way grudgingly to the set of rooms neatly landscaped up a slope overhung by scanty pine trees. Ronald Thwaite was annoyed.

Here they were, all 15 of them with their tour leader, Mr. Singh ('No, I am not a Sikh, I just have the surname Singh'). He was patient with the group, though beginning to fray half-way through their three-week tour of Rajastan.

'So many forts, or what are they called, "garhs"?' sighed Elizabeth Paignton.

'So many temples!' added Peter Baker.

'But think of Ranakpur, built at the same time as the dome of Florence cathedral . . .' Mr. Thwaite's rapid return interrupted Christine Wentworth's attempt to steer the comments towards more stirring cultural comparisons. A waiter rushed over to the flustered guest. 'Quick! There's something in her bed!' and he tossed over the keys to the hapless waiter who disappeared muttering, 'Monkeys, just monkeys.'

There were whole tribes of them in the pine trees, unnervingly surveying the humans below. As Christine's late husband had proposed to her under a tree in the park at Chatsworth, she knew how disconcerting it can be to have a peacock perching on a branch above; she was greatly concerned about unsolicited messages from the sky. Words floated into her mind, 'Thank God, cows don't fly!' as a sort of justification for the ways of creation.

'Mr. Singh, Mr. Singh, please go and have a look too,' the Thwaites shrilled.

'But I am come to inform you that the Land Rovers are ready to depart,' he persisted, frowning at what he considered was a request beyond his remit, 'Lodge people deal with your room, Mr. Thwaite,' he explained.

The waiter returned with the upper and under managers, both wringing their hands and bowing apologies to the Thwaites. Alicia began to moan, 'Monkeys! Horrible, flea-ridden sub-human creatures! They're not house-trained, by any wild chance?' For a few long moments the whole group sat contemplating the unthinkable: little grey wrinkled hands deftly turning the handles of their own bedroom doors.

'We'd better check we've locked the doors before we leave,' Peter advised, the first to break up the breakfasting group. Mr. Singh looked anxiously at his watch.

'Five minutes and we leave. Please be found at the reception.'

Shirley Constable, Christine's American friend, took her arm. 'We'd better check too.' She got up from the table, remarking that she wanted to clean her teeth, but then remembered they needed more bottled water. Gippy tummies provoked an undercurrent of anxiety in a group otherwise entranced by Rajastan. A country of extremes evoked simultaneous reactions, often divided by the spiritual and cerebral on one side, and the drearily physical on the other. That tribe of monkeys seemed oddly to unite the two.

The early morning sun was drying the air into spring warmth. Thatched hovels crouched below the road; women in purple, saffron yellow or deep blue saris were gathered round the village pump. The menfolk were working in the heavily-cultivated fields by a sluggish river as the first Land Rover turned towards the track winding up the wooded hill to the fort.

'Water-wheel!' was yelled back to the second vehicle where Mr. Singh perched strategically, preferring to survey his group in both directions, The first vehicle stopped, and out they jumped, cameras ready. The small river cut the sand into fresh morning eddies, and, as the wheel turned the water seemed to increase in volume, gushing out of the wooden frame with cool green-grey life-giving emphasis. A small boy eyed the row of pink-skins opposite him and stopped flicking his twig goad at the oxen. They paused, surveying the scene, muzzles raised, slowly blinking at the row of tourists as if summoned to a photo call, tails rhythmically hitting each dun flank though few flies gathered in the cool morning air. Six pairs of eyes querying 12 lenses. Christine moved towards Mr. Singh who was smoking a disgruntled cigarette, worried about the timing of the visit and the next destination. 'Could you give the little boy something from us, please? From our tipping kitty?' He nodded, but did nothing. A cry from the fields on the opposite bank, and the eight-year-old turned to whip the animals into motion. The liquid brown eyes, the water of life and the boy were now eternalised in twelve photographic memories.

Christine wanted to know more. As the Land Rovers resumed the climb and cultivated land petered out, she enquired, 'Who owns this land?' Mr. Singh had little time for landowners in this area.

'The same person who built the Lodge owns the fort and kilometres and kilometres of land.' Christine was surprised. She thought there had been land redistribution following Indian independence and Gandhi's ideals. Mr. Singh disagreed. He was a discontented man, forced to marry a daughter of his father's friend, instead of the wealthy heiress of an upwardly-mobile factory manager he had been assiduously courting. He had lost the dowry which might have set him up in business too. Being a tourist guide was neither lucrative nor appropriate for a graduate of Bombay University. His son wouldn't study but only indulged in sport – he didn't elaborate too much – and his daughter. Well, she studied conscientiously and was intelligent, but that didn't interest him much. His personal ambition was to set up a refuge in Bombay for young girls forced into prostitution and their children. Fine ideals, but strange how his daughter was edited out of his plans and emotions, Christine noted.

They had already visited two forts, but Kumbhalgarh was, as Mr. Singh had promised, rather special. The entrance tower soared into an uncanny silence in an over-populated, noisy land of restless contrasts. Mr. Singh herded his flock through the massive gate into the open area beyond, waiting to check all were there. He pointed to the hill of temples, peopling them with priests, pilgrims, soothsayers, warriors, craftsmen and labourers, ancestors of the impoverished children gathering around them. Oblivious of his increasing audience, Mr. Singh augmented his impassioned evocation, though his group hardly understood more than three words in five of his intoned English – the inhabitants of Kumbhalgarh could only follow his gestures and expressions, entranced.

The Mogul city inside the fort spread as far as the eye could see; thousands and thousands had once lived and worked inside the broad walls, wide enough for chariots to race behind the battlements. From the fort buildings (and here Mr. Singh told them to swing round and look up to a network of ramparts and crumbled towers) the Mogul emperor could see to the frontiers and beyond. Exhausted, Mr. Singh bowed his head, and went to sit on a dead trunk that had been placed specially for him, seer-like, in the shade of a storm-blasted tree. An awed silence, while the children and their elders sized up this group of foreigners. No woman, just the children, the kiosk keeper who doubled as the village overseer it seemed, while the village head, so Shirley and Christine decided, was the tall, handsome and rather scornful man eyeing them from the corner where the two alleys crossed.

The travellers drifted off towards the temples, led by the stout Thwaites and angular Paigntons. The children trotted after them, girls as well as boys, skin taking on a slightly luminescent look from the quartz in the dust, hands and feet prehensilely eloquent, eyes curious rather than pleading. Shirley and Christine followed behind the children, their exchanges poignantly enveloped by the hallowing silence.

'Pen, peni, pen, pen pen . . .' or so the children seemed to be crying out. Shirley emptied her purse of small change, and called –

'Hello!' They turned and ran back to her, palms out, eyes querying. She smiled and tried to give each a coin, but the hands moved and entangled one another. The subsequent squabbling made Shirley feel she had failed. Christine, having no change, took out a pack of pens she had brought with her. The sound of celluloid snapping and glint of a handful of pens sent the chorus into a higher key.

'Just like little monkeys!' announced Alicia Thwaite, looking back at them from the nearest temple. 'Peni, peni peni!' They didn't touch Christine or try to grab a pen. The quarrelling was reserved for the subsequent counting out of the spoils.

'What do they write on?' Christine wondered aloud as they turned their backs on the temples and started to walk up the wide chariot track to the fort. 'Should we have brought notepads with us too? Do they go to school, I wonder? I mean, what would they put on the paper?'

Shirley was equally puzzled. 'They could draw something.' A pause, as they thought back into the Mogul past, both enthralled and frightened.

'As these children are now, so were once our forebears?' Christine queried, wondering whether she took literacy too much for granted.

'The start of pictographs,' Shirley suggested.

'Signs or emblems, like the fish drawn in the sand by early Christians.'

'I suppose so.' Shirley considered the implications. 'We learn how to communicate by agreeing on meanings linked to shapes and signs . . . It's just primitive – or early – common sense.' The breeze took their words and offered them on the altars of space. Reaching the top of the fort the friends were so high up that the children of Kumbhalgarh became ants swarming over their hill; the Paigntons, Thwaites and the rest were still clambering spider-like over the temple ruins.

Christine felt a peace that she never imagined possible after her husband died. Shirley's anxieties ebbed away: she had taken a hasty break from her job in San Francisco to be with her friend after the funeral, and also to re-align her own job. Staff cuts were on the cards. Here it didn't seem to matter any more.

A lone figure was trudging up the dust track they had taken. It was Peter Baker.

'The others will be coming soon. I wanted to beat them to it. To taste the silence.' He smiled and sat a little apart from them in contemplation. Christine gazed at the wide ramparts. She had never imagined such fortifications could have been built, stretching for miles, winding over the upland plain to float out of mind into the mist of distance. There was space here, within those ramparts, for innumerable villages like the only remaining one below. For fields of produce, herds . . . Where did they find water on this upland plain? The water table couldn't be as low as the river they had passed, surely . . . She sketched in her mind the chariots careering along the ramparts. No need to have the 'garde-robes' in medieval castles here. People continued, presumably, then as now, to relieve themselves over the fields. It was all so vast that no one would notice, and, if they did, it was all in the course of things. Her mind wandered on from that to the native dress where there was no stitching to be done, no hems, yet, hey presto, openings were there in the places needed! All remained so dignified. A practical dignity.

The silence sculpted her thoughts. Silence so monumental that, vertically or horizontally, it was endless; it flowed into the pores to the quick of one's identity, clear, colourless, no scent nor sound, only the sight of things as disembodied as the birds, vultures or eagles, circling silent specks of transmigrating souls. Christine gazed out into the recesses of space and time, to the 13th-century when all this would have been newly built. By slaves? Or peasants? Then she drew birds and fish and simple chariots with the end of the stick she always carried when climbing to ward off her ancestral fear of snakes. Shirley looked at her for a while, relieved her friend was becoming reconciled to her loss.

'The others are arriving.' They hadn't noticed Peter standing by them.

Christine waved to the rest of the group as she and Shirley passed them on the way up as they began the descent. She already had her plans in place. They found the tense and sinewy Mr. Singh was refreshing himself at the makeshift hut serving as a rudimentary general store. Christine made for him.

'Could you get permission for me to look inside one of the houses? Please? I'll pay whatever you suggest,' Mr. Singh frowned at her for a while, then turned to the village shopkeeper, who was rearranging bottles of tepid lemonade.

'In a moment. He will ask.' Christine waited as patiently as she could. She didn't want the rest of the group to return and follow her.

The shop was on one side of the open space opposite the massive gateway and close to a narrow alley barely wide enough for two slim bodies to pass. Children were running and jumping between doorless entrances and walls of animal pens on the other side of the alley. A goat wandered across their path; the muzzle of a cow sniffed at a few dry leaves pushed towards it. No hens. Christine worried whether the scrawny cows could produce enough milk, penned into that tiny space, with no sign of hay or fodder. Just cow-dung moulded into pancake shapes, laid in the sun to dry, and stacked in neat cone-shaped piles. Nothing wasted here.

'Lucky they are to see one egg in ten days,' pronounced Mr. Singh at her shoulder. 'He would be the first to be offered it.' 'He' was the tall, soberly impressive man she had picked out earlier as the village leader, now leading them down another identical alley, past more goats, cowpat hives, soft fly-encrusted bovine nostrils and hollow tawny flanks; past the stench of urine mingled with the smell of burning. He didn't choose to look at her; his eyes scanned the upland plain, as he stood sentry by an opening into a dwelling of sorts, one hand motioning Mr. Singh and Christine into the dark.

She sensed the smile before she saw it. There it was, a little tentative, lingering by the tiny flames curling round a small fire of sun-dried cowpats supporting a wide shallow pan. A woman was squatting, kneading dough, her purple sari clutched by a little child at her knee. Christine put her hands together and bowed her head, whispering that she was honoured to be allowed in. Perhaps the tone of her voice conveyed her thanks, for the head man's wife stood up and opened her hand in a gentle gesture towards the seat of honour, a tree trunk, apparently the only piece of furniture. She continued putting the bread on the hot metal, and Christine asked Mr. Singh to express her thanks. Even the mildest of smalltalk seemed utterly inappropriate – how long have you lived here? How many children have you? What are they doing? . . . They would be trivial even intrusive enquiries amid this struggle for survival. Mr. Singh led her into the inner room, bare beyond imagination. Some crooked branches had been embedded in the walls; on them hung a couple of striped threadbare blankets, a folded sari, and a long wide, off-white strip of material. Perhaps it was an unwound *dhoti*?

'Where do they sleep?'

Mr. Singh looked at the floor, the branches, and at Christine before he answered, 'Here. On the floor.'

'What's it made of? It doesn't look like earth.'

'Cow dung. It is patted on everything. In the hot season, it comes less hot; in the cool season, it is warm. It is cleaner –' Christine winced in unthinking amazement '– than dust or sand, and they have a rug to lie on, warm in winter, cool in summer.'

Smile answered smile again as they left; the child at the young woman's knee just stared at Christine, too young to 'pen, peni' her yet.

The others were back and waiting for them by the dilapidated shop where a few had bought bottles of lemonade to wash down the packed lunches provided by the Lodge.

'Couldn't you have taken us too?' Alicia Thwaite voiced her thoughts with a touch of petulance. Shirley laughed, pointing out that these folk might be humble and desperately poor, but they didn't lack dignity, and would hardly have liked all 16 to crowd into their tiny mud hut. Christine glanced her thanks across to Shirley as they all traipsed after Mr. Singh to the Land Rovers.

'Why don't we walk back to the Lodge?' Shirley whispered to Christine. 'We can share the silence, forget the others, gather our impressions. It's all downhill and only a couple of miles at the most.'

They set off, rapt in their own thoughts which gradually criss-crossed into discussion, being the people they were.

'I wish I could do something,' Christine burst out. 'They have nothing, absolutely nothing. We talk of "the bare essentials", but we haven't a clue what it actually means. These people haven't even the bare essentials. They look so lean and hungry, and the animals look the same, And why aren't there any vegetable patches?'

'Where's the water?' Shirley asked rhetorically. 'The river is miles away, and I didn't see any sign of a well.'

'Mr. Singh told us that tens of thousands were living inside that fort centuries ago, after the Mogul invasions, They must have had water. So either the water table has fallen, or water was brought up in barrels – somehow.'

'Haven't we forgotten the rain?' suggested Shirley. 'It seems so dry, but there is a rainy season and the monsoon waters could have been gathered in underground cisterns. If they could build those ramparts and had chariots, they must have had draught animals. Digging cisterns and lining them with stones would have been child's play.'

They walked on in silence, their pace quickening in unison with their thoughts. The sun was touching the rim of the valley and the early evening bird and animal cries drifted out of the woods. Thin curls of smoke marked the village lower down the valley.

Christine was worrying away at the visible lack of vegetables. 'I asked Mr. Singh, and he said they were sent every week from the Punjab. How do they pay for them up at Kumbhalgarh? They don't seem to have anything that could serve as a cash crop. Did you see any sort of cultivation?'

'No,' Shirley agreed. 'It crossed my mind the people at Kumbhalgarh might have to survive by foraging. Strange, though – they're only about three miles away from those rice fields by the river.'

'Precisely,' Christine insisted. 'There's no water in the fort area. Mr. Singh says the fort and the paddy fields are owned by the same person, who makes no attempt to improve things for the inhabitants of the fort. No school, yet those children implore us to give them pens rather than pennies.'

'That's the tragedy of it all,' Shirley said, almost in tears. 'Those children, they're so full of energy, even a sort of hope, with their little hands grasping these pens. But they can't write. So what is there to hope for? Semi-starvation at best, depending on the weather?'

'That owner – he might at least provide a hut for a school!' Christine blurted out in frustration. 'My dream would be to pay for someone to go away and be educated – say the man with the shop. He can't be more than 30 . . . On the condition he would have to come back and teach all of those children, girls as well as boys, so they could have a chance. Each person sent away to study would then return to teach the younger ones, and so on; the teaching carries on, opportunities are given. The children could study the latest agricultural methods . . .' Christine paused because Shirley was peering down the road.

'What are you looking out for?' Christine asked.

'For the nearest electricity line. It's probably at the Lodge, but that's owned by the local Rajah or whatever. He could run a line up to the fort for a computer terminal. No use education without technology. The world of the future.'

Christine stopped short and looked at Shirley in amazement. 'If this Rajah or whoever were persuaded to put electricity in the fort, then what about a pump for the well, and communal showers, as well as proper irrigation, and, well, no point having a computer terminal if there isn't someone to use it and teach how to. Aren't we guilty of putting lots of horses in front of the cart which isn't even in sight?'

They started walking again even faster. Turning the corner to the village they saw women with pitchers drawing the evening supply of water. Not a chimney was without smoke, and Christine looked knowingly at the artistically arranged cowpat pyramids. She recalled the dough kneaded beside that tiny fire, and again the lack of vegetables for these vegetarians angered her. 'They don't even seem to use cow dung for manuring crops; it has to be used for fuel and building material.'

The Lodge was further than they had reckoned, nearly four miles below the fort.

'Mr. Singh did tell me a couple of days ago,' Christine confided as they strode on, 'how much it would cost to sink a well and buy enough land for a family to feed and shelter itself, and even save a bit to hitch itself a rung or two up the ladder.' She paused, remembering how distressed she had felt. 'I was carrying more than that amount around with me in my bag. In cash. I felt like running out, grabbing the first adult I saw, and then say, "Here, take this and dig a well, buy cattle, and" . . .'

'Complications, always complications,' Mr. Singh sighed later that evening to the two would-be reformers. 'No one would return to a place like Kumbhalgarh once he got out and was educated and could make much money elsewhere. If it's not human nature, I can tell you it's Indian nature,' he affirmed with the decisiveness of a guru. He started to get up from the easy chair in the hotel reception area.

'No, Mr. Singh. Please wait a moment!' Shirley cried out.

They had him pincered between them. He sank back in the chair with a murmur, defeated. 'Why should the owner provide a proper water supply when the villagers owe him so much money already which they can never repay even in two lives?' They were puzzled by the last phrase, but Mr. Singh was a Hindu.

'Owe him so much money?' they responded together. Mr. Singh leant back, clasped his hands over his knees, and explained the villagers were 'tribals', and would have had to borrow to buy a cow or a goat. They had water from the monsoon and a very shallow well which dried up most years. The water table had fallen steadily for centuries. The landowner said they had to repay the loan taken out to buy the

9

cow, or goat, before he could provide a better well, or even that undreamed of luxury, electricity, or even a school hut because who would pay the teacher?

'Didn't they pay back the loan?'

'The landowner knew they never would, never could when he made the loan. What money can they make? From tourists like you who pay to look into a house? They have nothing to sell. In India women carry stones on the road because they are cheaper than men, both cheaper than tractors.'

'Little better than slaves,' Christine murmured. 'Bonded labour.'

A life's imprisonment. It served the owner, who felt he had done his bit by the loan, and 'enough was enough'. People were told to pull themselves up by their bootstraps, but if they hadn't any boots? Economic, social, human desolation, as profound as the silence that engulfed them at the highest point of the fort. It was like a Gray's *Elegy* in an Indian fort, except they were buried alive in their youth without hope.

'No world is their oyster. They can never have a chance to achieve,' Shirley reflected, looking at the first delicate strokes of the sunset on the Indian pine trees descending the slope outside the Lodge. 'Words fail me. My heart bleeds to think of them, like animals, waking in the morning to see how they can live through the day, provide food of sorts, a fire to cook at least, and shelter. They need the cow for the cowpats almost as much as for the milk.' It was survival at its most basic, involving waking thoughts of how to survive the day, with a bitter reckoning at sundown. Hunger, half or hardly assuaged, would be further burdened by the chain of a lifetime's debt, the inheritance of the children of Kumbhalgarh. Contrite souls, they wept inwardly, through frustration and guilt and the pity of it all.

'Small starts,' Mr. Singh murmured, 'can work. Very slowly.' He paused and looked at the pines where a chattering tribe of monkeys had congregated. 'A goat is given to a family. A charity supplies the money. That goat, which is looked after by a young child, is female and given to that charity's he-goat. Then when two little ones are born, one is returned as payment, the other kept by the family. With their first, female one, of course. The next time they can sell one goat, and, if there is more than one, then it must go back to the charity. The female ones returned are given out to more families, the male ones used to produce more little goats, or sold. That could start here. Small starts.'

All three sank into silent reflection. Christine could see the Thwaites and Paigntons ordering whiskey at the bar across the reception area.

'Too slow,,' Shirley broke the silence. 'Think of those lives lost forever. An Einstein, a Beethoven, a Shakespeare, a . . . the pity of it all.'

'Goats need water and don't produce vegetables. The families at the fort doesn't even have a fruit tree, bananas or something . . . ' Christine's voiced trailed into silence at the realisation of her abject ignorance of what could be expected to grow, let alone thrive, in this climate, and at the altitude of the fort.

'Cash,' Mr. Singh uttered succinctly. He slowly leant forward and stood up, as if still thinking, and pulled down the sleeves of his immaculately-laundered blue-striped shirt. 'I still prefer direct action. Charities are corrupt. Better give blankets to people than charities. I shall one day get a place in Bombay for young girls who sell themselves, and for their children. Give them a way to earn. Perhaps never, because I, too, am poor.'

Shirley knew that he, the driver and the sweeper slept in the coach. All the hotels would do, she surmised, was to launder their clothes, let them wash, or perhaps take a shower. She had noticed the rugs and cushions discreetly stored away on the bumpy rear seats no one wanted.

'Too little, too late,' Christine lamented, trembling though the air was mild. She thought of those children on their haunches round the cowpat fire, eating whatever the day and their parents' toil had to offer. She recalled the inner beauty of their smiles, their 'pen, peni' chatter, their slim, thin bodies glistening with the luminescent dust of centuries, and their lack of resentment. No graceless surliness here.

'Look at Mr. Singh. A degree from Bombay University, and a bundle of unfulfilled aspirations, unhappy in his family and in his job, even though he has just been appointed to a higher post. He's frustrated, embittered, caught in the relentless rat race of the educated, but with a heart for more than money. Maybe the children would be happier left in ignorance?'

Shirley stared at her amazed. 'What price choice, or human values? There must be a difference between human bondage, and animal bondage.'

Alicia Thwaite waddled over with her drink to plump herself down where Mr. Singh had been sitting. She pointed at the monkeys chattering in the pine trees, and shuddered, sipped herself into calmness again and commented on the children of Kumbhalgarh. Wasn't it strange that they wanted pens, of all things, and how scraggy and grubby they were?

'Just like little animals!' declared Mrs. Alicia Thwaite.

for Susan

PLASTIC BAGS

It began long ago with sand and sandwiches. Her young family objected to sand-crunchy sandwiches, so she wrapped them more carefully and remembered to use one plastic carrier bag for beach equipment, and the other for food and drink. In those days shops only supplied plain white ones with a black design, so Jenny provided herself with sticky labels and thick black pens for identification purposes. Her two sons and daughter would never erase the image of their mother holding up innumerable plastic bags and spinning them round till she found the label.

'Wouldn't it be quicker to peep inside, Mummy?' they suggested with knowing looks all round.

'Yes,' she thought, 'but that's not the way my recognition reflexes work.'

There was never enough space in her working den for the books that jostled with paper files and sewing boxes, water-colours and attempts at basket-weaving, begun, abandoned or waiting for a decision to scrap or renew. Piles of exercise books awaited attention together with attempts to produce an effective tax filing system. A file marked 'Very Urgent' spewed its contents onto the floor across half-sorted papers. No, files were no longer adequate. The local stationer's had introduced red plastic carrier bags; they were to contain and control matters financial. Red, a danger signal, demanding attention.

Blue carrier bags soon followed, mainly from the local department store, shortly joined by the bright green of 'Marks and Sparks'. Blue was for the art history notes, green for philosophy, and what about yellow? Yellow was for sunshine and holiday brochures. All these colours danced an uncoordinated waltz with the tartan curtains and pale green walls of her study. Jenny found peace in their reassuringly organised colour code.

Tony, her elder son, had sent them a postcard of Raphael's *School of Athens* during a school trip to Rome. She kept it on her desk as it reminded her how, as a child, she would run out of the wood where her parents and brother were picking bluebells onto the open hillside, up and up the slope towards the beckoning skyline. She'd be called back, 'Jenny, it's time to go. Jenny, it's getting dark . . . cold . . . late . . .' but she had to reach the brow of the hill, however distant, look over, know what lay beyond; only then could she trot back, head bowed ready for the inevitable reproaches. 'Jenny, why are you so disobedient . . . difficult . . . deaf . . ?'

She couldn't explain her overwhelming need to see, to control what lay out of sight – over the hill, beyond Raphael's arches and the philosophers under them – to overcome her fear of future unseen. The chores waiting to be done felt more manageable in their colour-allotted plastic carrier bags. She doubted her family would understand because it all sounded rather silly.

So what had Raphael's sublime masterpiece to do with running up to the brow of the hill or even with plastic bags, you may well ask. It was only a fresco covering a wall in the Vatican with groups of debating philosophers, a half-naked white-bearded figure, probably some sort of soothsayer, straddling the steps below the coffered arches and their stern stone commentators, the statues in the niches. Jenny loved the groups of students at the front, said to be portraits of the colony of artists working in Rome centuries ago for Pope Julius II but, to her, companion souls. One was bending elegantly over a text; another, further back, writing in a book supported on his crooked leg; yet another scribbling excitedly on paper placed against the plinth of a column that rose above a real doorway in the papal apartments. Platonic or Aristotelian, their minds quickened their bodies, the exhilaration of learning hallowed by the arches above them, soaring like their spirits into the snatches of blue sky. Look carefully, and the arches appeared to turn their undersides with coffering, rosettes and carved intricacies towards her. There must be a prospect on the other side.

She imagined herself running up those steps, oblivious to all the calls: 'Jenny there is the meal to prepare, Simon has a music lesson, Tony and Laura have homework, you have essays to correct, come back, time's running out . . .' But on she strode, side-stepping the seer whose prophetic tones seemed to echo in her imagination, waving at her favourite youth on the right, who continued writing intently in his notebook, up past Plato and Aristotle propounding and their guardian statues surveying, on and over to see what . . . That's where she was always interrupted: a phone call, a knock on the door of her den, or Thomas with, 'Time to wake up, Jenny,' a cup of tea and a

Raphael. *The School of Athens*

frustratingly loving kiss. Thomas, her husband, the innocent slayer of her dreams, not only tolerated, but even encouraged her use of plastic bags.

'If it makes you happy, darling.' She would frown back at him.

'Not exactly happy. More settled. A feeling that I won't lose bills or somebody's homework quite so easily . . .'

'Good. It's a fine system,' he agreed, not listening at all. His approach was unsystematic and relaxed, even untidy. He actually lost the income tax forms they stress are 'not replaceable if you lose them,' and a telephone bill, including the final reminder in red, so the line was cut to bitter recriminations all round. Especially from the younger generation, two of them teenagers by then.

Laura, the elegant female of the family, was the most scornful about the plastic carrier bags. Jenny had resigned herself to this. For each successive Christmas her daughter asked pointedly for the most up-to-the-minute filofax. She proudly flaunted her efficient way of carrying all the information she required in her sleek black organiser of the moment. Jenny suspected that her daughter found her wispy, disorganised, dowdy in her comfortable skirts and shoes and generally in need of an image fix. Needless to say, the plastic bags were part of that general daughterly disapproval.

Laura didn't understand that her mother had problems with the hour. There were just not enough minutes to organise all her needs into pert little systems, because of the time required to decode an error, or even, Jenny feared, to notice it. When a couple of rails crossed in her many-track mind, then she would think of the right colour and pull the bag down from the shelf or cupboard top. Her strategy was to check pages from a chosen bag to identify matters that had matured into a scream for urgent action – to be rapidly transferred to the red plastic bag. The bags always seemed to invade the hollow of the night, leading to endless futile cogitations as to whether she would recall this or that pressing matter in the morning. Would it be wiser to click on the light without waking Thomas, write it down and hurl the paper where she could not fail to walk over it and absorb its warning on her way to the bathroom? Jenny couldn't face the imagined complications of keying these urgent matters into the neat memory machine that organised Laura's life.

It all became a sort of family joke, edged with criticism. However untidy he was himself, Jenny knew from the look of disdain that crossed Thomas's face that he found the plastic bags slovenly, unaesthetic and constantly escaping out of their designated areas – the kitchen and his wife's study – into his own. Humour relieved his irritation. Jenny never forgot that unique Sunday morning when the children actually got up before she did, invaded her bedroom where she was happily propped up reading the newspaper, and cried in unison – did she glimpse Thomas conducting them with glee from the back? – 'What are you organising for us today, Mummy? What's your programme? Which colour bags – and are you sure you know what is in which? Slip in some yellow pleasure ones, please, not just dark-coloured duty!'

For her birthday Tony and Simon would give her plastic bags of the most outrageous, or handsome, designs they could find. Jenny loved this more than she dared admit. A beautiful waxy bag with a Monet painting or a William Morris design meant that she couldn't desecrate it with a label; only very special files were entrusted to such bags. Sometimes they were just neatly folded and put in the 'special occasions' zone in her study, to gather dust.

They were not exactly a small family, so Jenny would take provisions as gifts in her 'art' plastic bags on those longed-for weekends when they were invited to stay with friends. Sandwiches would go in the supermarket blue and green ones, followed by others containing her work for the journey.

'The blue and red by my feet in the front passenger seat, Tony, please. The art ones in the boot with the suitcases. Not too many, or they'll think we're descending on them for a month! The supermarket blue and green ones in the back with you, in case you get hungry. We're already late and can't stop on the way.' Moans from the back seat, with Thomas winking in their direction. Jenny would feel better after adding scattered sheets to the income tax in the red carrier bag, essays for next Monday to the blue one, unread newspapers to the purple one, while catalogues that still cascaded through the letter box, in spite of her having ticked all the 'no unsolicited publicity' boxes she could find, were stuffed into another scruffy white one.

'Why don't you just chuck them out? Or better, send them back and say you must be taken off the mailing list?' Thomas suggested, but if they came, she just had to look at them. The urge was too strong for her to do anything except put them in a bag, marked with a label or colour-coded.

As a child, Jenny had scanned the hedgerows for dandelions to feed her pet rabbits, which propagated rapidly. Her mother just told her they 'would have to go and see Mr. Conisbee the butcher, such a nice man'. They never came back. She could still feel the pleasure of twisting the thick leaves until the yellow-white juice came out, so good for her pets, she thought. So she fed them, cleaned out their hutches and stroked their sleek fur. In some unfathomable way they reassured her. That is, until they left to visit Mr. Conisbee. She often thought of them as she straightened or rearranged the ever -increasing number of plastic carrier bags, a multi-coloured bastion against the confusion of scattered sheets, the rush of unfettered time, the unobtrusive, slithery betrayal of the future, too soon become frighteningly present.

It was Jenny's idea to go to India. She had been talking about it for years, so much so that Thomas was convinced it would remain safely in the fertile realm of her imagination. No such luck. She saved up, paid for his tour as well as hers, and organised a band of friends; it was a long-standing dream about to come true. Thomas grumbled at the prospect of endlessly changing hotels, the constant packing and unpacking, suspecting she had some scheme which she was keeping to herself. He was not surprised when the day for packing arrived to be handed a pile of different coloured plastic bags, all labelled: 'shirts, long-sleeved', 'shirts, short-sleeved', 'underpants', 'vests', 'socks', 'ties', and so on. 'Never take anything out of them except to wear, and never put anything in them that needs washing. There's no need to unpack, you see. You just follow the colour code, your own. Mine is different.' She usually became flustered at departures, but now, confident in this system, she radiated tranquil delight.

'What if I don't remember the colour code and have to grope inside the bags?' She smiled sweetly and handed him three cards explaining the code:

'One for your wallet, one for the top of your suitcase, the third in case you lose one of the other cards. It's your reserve.'

Thomas hoped that as the years passed, so would her frantic need for the plastic bags to control her space and time. He gave her a smart purple and blue Liberty design bag. She loved it and confessed that she felt better turned-out with it, and hoped that Laura would approve. To Thomas's dismay, the Liberty bag replaced not only two of the three or four plastic bags she had taken everywhere for years to supplement her capacious handbag but, also, the handbag itself. Was there no end to the way these bags displaced other useful objects but defiantly remained *in situ* as if tablets of stone?

For many years, probably starting about the time of that Sunday incident when the children taunted her about the plastic bags, Jenny had been dreaming of a funeral. It didn't bother her waking hours as the whole scene was not an unhappy one. To begin with, it was sunny.

Children were kicking a ball around behind the people, mostly friends and family, who were following a coffin down some generalised leafy Surrey lane. The vicar was at the lych-gate of a Norman church. Suddenly there was a commotion. Somebody had been left behind, or was late. Her familiar territory. Then she saw herself running madly to catch up with the procession, waving the Liberty bag and, inevitably, a rainbow of plastic carrier ones, at least five she reckoned. People at the back stopped, and tapped the shoulders of those in front of them. They all stepped aside to let Jenny reach the coffin. Up went the lid and one of the bearers gave her a leg-up. In she popped, pulling the array of bags after her. The red one got caught as the lid closed. Up the lid came again, and Jenny saw herself smiling, as usual apologetically, as she hauled in her offending bag, the 'matters urgent' one. At this point in the dream Thomas would turn and wink at Laura, Tony and Simon, who shrugged their shoulders. Those bags again!

for Maurice, John and Diane

ON BURYING THE DEAD

I am Katia, twenty-six years old, and born in Leningrad like my mother. But my *babushka* was born in St. Petersburg, and she met the Tsar whose remains we are expecting. I think this is a good wall to sit on, in this oldest part of our city, the fortress. We can see Peter and Paul cathedral and statue of Peter the Great.

You want to know what I think about this burial of the Tsar? As I pass the Lenin statues, I tell you, 'Let them stay. It's history.' We must live with history. That is what Lenin's arm pointing out, finger down, stern look say. Yes, it is good, important, not to forget.

So here are the Romanovs, some of the last Romanovs, coming back to Saint Petersburg, dead. But it has returned to the name they knew 80 years ago when they lived. Only by a small, very small majority, but the people of Leningrad did vote to have the old name back.

Yes, Nicholas II did talk to my grandmother, and she never forgot. I think her spirit is waiting with us now, happy. She was always telling me, her one grandchild, how lovely to be addressed by him. Yes, the Tsar visited her school, in Saint Petersburg, because it was founded by some his relation, perhaps a Tsaritsa, or as you say, Tsarina. Perhaps, yes, your Queen Victoria's grand-daughter Alexandria. She married Tsar Nicholas II, and after the coronation in Moscow, a terrible thing happened. In the meadow outside the city where there was a big celebratory feast, thousands rushed towards the food and beer, crushing many others to death in the mud, face down. A bad omen, yes. You, the first ever, asked me why all Tsar tombs in Peter and Paul Cathedral the same? All re-done on the orders of Tsar Alexander in 1865, I am told, but not his own tomb. That is different and much, much grander. His and his wife's took 17 years to cut, carve, polish. Now the new ones for Tsar Nicholas II and the Tsaritsa will be there, but I do not know how they will be.

Why bury them 80 years later, to the very day, you ask me? Perhaps even not the true bones. Some descendants of the Romanovs say no, they don't come today. Others do think they are true relics, all Tsar, Tsaritsa, three daughters and three servants. Missing, another daughter, Maria, and the Tsarevich Alexei. Maybe bodies burnt 80 years ago by Bolsheviks. But I did go to study biology at university and I understand the DNA experts from Britain, Russia, USA too, all agree they are the true Romanovs. Agree on Romanovs. Yes. How, you ask? I think matching their hair with hair in love lockets. And Prince Philip's, and others'.

No, I stopped biology. No work in biology after Berlin wall fall, and *perestroika*. Mother was history teacher, and lost her job because she did not teach the right things. The history she was to teach always changing. Now she has little pension, too little to buy anything at the store you asked me to show you, near the blocks of flats along the road past the Victory Monument.

So here history brings up the funeral of the Tsar who spoke to my very grandmother. Yes, he was kind. She never forgot his kindness. 'Just like one of us!' she repeated. 'But so polite. Very quiet.' My grandmother dead in 1983. In 1983 aged 82. She never forgot the Tsar, like someone very special, but she could not say exactly why. He was not a tall man. Just nice. My mother was *babushka*'s third child, born in Leningrad in 1938 in the Great Terror, but *babushka* knew nothing about Stalin's purges. She believed it was sad necessity to remove dissidents obstructing Russia's great future for everyone.

Babushka spoke little of the Bolshevik revolution. Yes, our tragic Civil War during World War I. It had to be. Mother speaks a lot. Nicholas II was very, very bad, she says. He allowed a lot of people, poor people, to be killed. It was a cold, cold January in 1905; there were 150,000 men, women and children peacefully marching from all parts of the city carrying portraits of Tsar Nicholas and singing hymns. They were going to the Winter Palace to ask him for more, how do you say, civil rights, fairer labour laws, for example. For no reason he ordered the Imperial Guards to fire on them. Many, maybe more than a thousand, were killed. 'Bloody Nicholas' he was known, my mother always says. This Tsar still refused the civil rights, until his uncle, Grand Duke Nicholas, put pistol to his head. 'Sign this new constitution, or I shoot.' The Tsar signed, but things did not get better. My grandparents met at this time, as now, with shops empty and fear of famine.

Now everybody at Moscow looking at the family photographs of the last Tsar. He loved his wife so much. *Babushka* said he loved the people, but my mother always added, if she heard, that he only loved his people if they loved him and did as he wanted. Nicholas was 16,

Alexandra 12, when they met. Ten years passed by, and they married. All those four little girls, then Alexei. At last, a boy, but so ill.

Nobody knew why the poor little boy was so ill. You tell me your Queen Victoria passed on, how do you say it, haemophilia? We were told it was a punishment for their wickedness. But in Moscow they only see a happy family, always smiling in the sun. He loved his wife, his family, his people – as long as they loved him and behaved as he wanted them to.

You are interested in Rasputin? Oh, he is very Russian. Our history is full of 'holy fools', who think they see the future for important people. They all are poor, passionate and in some way sort of crazy, never stupid. There was one outside the old stone house where my grandfather was very ill, overlooking the Griboedov Canal by the Lion Bridge, with a pediment over the big entrance and sculpture on it, all worn out now, empty and decaying. He was telling of the end of the siege of Leningrad, of how the people would rise again, of the spirit of Lenin who was there guiding us. Lenin, the heroic founder of the People's Republic, a kind man who really cared about the workers and did not sign orders to kill thousands as Nicholas II did.

So did Stalin, you tell me. My *babushka* did not know this. She was having her three children and working at the same time. She was too tired to know much. She told me he, Stalin, was a great leader guiding us into a better, richer, juster future. The future of a Great Power. And she believed him, then. He was her hope. And my mother's, at first.

It is July now, summer and hot, but you cannot believe how cold it gets in winter. Yes, the snow arrives in October even, and stays up to April. Up to April, yes. The snow froze the dead bodies – people, animals – during the 900 days of the German blockade, so perhaps that was a good. No plague. Winter defeats the armies that invade us. Napoleon, then Hitler. But Russian people always resist enemies from outside.

Babushka was quiet about her youth. She met my grandfather in the countryside at the family *dacha*. In late spring they left Petrograd – Saint Petersburg had been given a more Russian name at the time of the war against the Kaiser – for Peterhof where there was an old house, perhaps 18th-century, destroyed during the Nine Hundred Days. *Babushka* used to tell me of the journey out to the countryside beginning with the blossom dancing still in her eyes as it did long ago, every spring. They had some land, and peasants grew vegetables. She remembers picking fruit in the summer, scent of the flowers, woods so green they became blue at the horizon, and rowan berries in autumn. So many berries, orange, yellow, blood red, came in autumn. Which was when she met my grandfather. His family had a *dacha* nearby.

They had to wait so long to get married because of the World War and then the Revolution. They had little money. Russia had to rebuild for the people after the war devastation. That is why there were no children for so long. My mother was only three at her earliest memory of the Russian 'holy fool' who chanted outside our home where her father was dying of hunger, in the Nine Hundred Days.

Yes, I told you my mother has a *dacha*. It is not the same one where *Babushka* met grandfather. That was taken to give to the people at the Revolution, I think. No, my mother has a piece of land and a hut. She goes there to grow vegetables, and to smell the countryside. It is not long here the growing period in this region. Vegetables, and fruit, are expensive. Very expensive.

Babushka never forgot the Tsar. She went to Saint Nicholas cathedral I showed you near the Mariinskiy Theatre. There she had my mother baptised, secretly. *Babushka* took me there; too had me baptised, I think without telling my mother. Churches we were told were monuments to the great work of Russian craftsmen. It was not easy to find one for a baptism, but *Babushka* did.

What are the people near us saying? They are curious, like you, to see what will happen. Nothing like this has happened in their life. Lenin, then Stalin, were given big, big funerals, state funerals I think you say. This is not the same. This funeral is private. The Patriarch of the Russian Orthodox Church is not coming still. But our President Yeltsin now is.

Have I seen Lenin's mausoleum? Yes, once, with a school group. No, Stalin had gone from there before I was born. Well, we stood in a long, long queue winding all round Red Square on a cold bright day in May. We were told to be silent and serious as if at a funeral in great history. It was like walking along a clear path of destiny to meet and honour the man who made it possible – we were not quite sure what. The sun was shining, but it was cold outside. There were soldiers who had to stand so very still for so many hours. Then inside it was all so dark and smooth, sort of red granite, so hard, like going into an Egyptian tomb. The interior, it was cold stillness. You know. You have been there in Moscow. Except no queue, you say, only two soldiers. Did Lenin wear a suit and spotted necktie when I went? I cannot remember, but, yes, he did look a bit like a waxwork, under the spotlight. People were weeping, older ones. Some of our school group

24

too, not really knowing what to do. You see, we were told he had saved our country from the tyranny of money, from slavery to the owners of land, of industry. From your capitalism that exploited the workers.

My father met my mother in 1958 when he was told to stand by her in the endless queue. Everyone had to be in pairs, and only speak softly. They were only 20 then. For a long time they were whispering until at last they saw their hero Stalin beside Lenin, Stalin who had saved their country, encouraged industry, science, technology and the great space programme of Russian science. They believed it would all lead to our glorious future. But then there was Khrushchev, and three years later, before people realised, Stalin's body was out.

Russian people here have come to look, like you, not feeling it is really part of their history. Tsar Nicholas lived so long ago and in what appears like another country to them. For better, some think: for worse, others. A few will make the sign of the cross, some may kneel, the older people.

* * * * *

So what now, you are asking? The slow procession: the silent people watching. Some people of the Russian Orthodox Church in exile want Tsar Nicholas II to be made holy martyr. Now the remains are just called the 'servants of the Lord', as the Patriarch in Moscow is not sure these are the true bones. They cannot, on his orders, be named. Yeltsin changed his mind – yes, again! – just so history will tell he is here today! Perhaps he is thinking of what to do with Lenin's body, you are asking me? He Lenin himself wanted, he wrote, a quiet funeral in Petrograd, to be buried with his mother. Anyway, what did he do really to save our country? *Babushka* and my grandfather met when the shops were empty, like now, and they believed Lenin would change all that forever. Now we have Yeltsin who jumped on the tank to stop bloodshed, brought Western capitalism, and the food shops are empty again!

I do not understand and am confused like most of the people around here. Only, as I told you, a few tears from the old, a few crossing themselves and trying to kneel. If *babushka* had been here, she would have crossed herself, knelt if she could, but then she would have been too old, at 97. Yes, ninety-seven. But she would weep, yes, a river of weeping, to, 'Oh, the Tsar was so kind, so polite!' My grandfather I only remember like a shadow. Very serious. very sad. He would have watched and shaken his head. He died so long ago. Not old. Forty-three, during the Nine Hundred Days. His last daughter, my mother, is now at home and angry. She is angry about

25

what she calls, in Russian, 'the death of hope'. 'There is no future!' she says. 'It is all problems, no money, nothing to build on. Everyone for themselves. No feeling of working to a purpose in common,' or something like that. She often sits moaning in *babushka's* rocking-chair, 'What did my father die for? Like all the millions of others? The soldiers? What did we all suffer for, and us here in Leningrad, for nine hundred days, more than most?' And she will go on and on so that I leave the flat, to the sound of her curses on the 'spivs' I think you call them, or 'mafia' or the cheating people who want all. The 'sons of capitalism', she calls them. Of lots of money for a few, and the devil take the rest! So the people who work have no money because they are not paid, and the people without work have no money because they do no work, and the pensions are so small that in winter my mother has not enough for food. So I left biology for the Tourist school, to help them with money.

Do you wait now they are all in Peter and Paul Cathedral? Yes, we wait. You ask how I feel about waiting. I feel unquiet spirits around me in this fortress. So many have not been put to rest. Behind the Cathedral near the Boathouse where you went to the shop, there the Bolsheviks shot four grand dukes, one of them a writer of history who did not write what they said was true, and other hostages. It was 1919. The Tsars all used isolated prison cells also. You saw the best. I could not go with you. They whisper their history about torture there of revolutionaries against the Tsars, dissidents against the Bolsheviks, put into cells you are not shown. Below the water level. Damp solitude: no visitors, no books, only guards who crept along carpeted corridors to spy on their nameless prisoners. No visitors, no books, for years on end. Solitary confinement you tell me, yes, with solitary bath and exercise once every 14 days. Some went crazy. Many died of despair. Peter the Great killed his son, the Tsarevich Alexei, in the Gosudarev Bastion behind us. This fortress was built by forced labour. Thousands died. We are standing on an island of blood.

Did I not tell you of my father? He is ill, depressed and silently longing for the old days. He usually is out. Before he was engineer in state factory. A job and security after much study and wait. He came from a peasant family, joined the Communist Party, was sent to university to be engineer. He wanted his job and did not believe all the bad stories in Khrushchev's time about his hero, Stalin. He, like his wife, lost people from his family during the Nine Hundred Days. Leningrad was freed in January, 1944, and 16 months later glorious Russian troops were in Berlin. It was Stalin who led us then. He wanted to believe, to hope, not to know that Stalin was killing thousands, some say millions, in the Great Terror just when they were both born, the year of 1938. Father wanted his job. They wanted a family. So he was silent, worked, went to Party meetings. My mother was history teacher. First she believed all she was teaching. Lenin was the first Soviet hero, then Stalin, both working for a juster, greater future for Russia where women were liberated, could do jobs the same as men. This was true with Communism, do you know? Then she was made to change the message. Stalin became bad overnight. So she did not tell my father, but began to meet dissidents and then write *samizdat*. You know what that is? No. Writing about civil rights by poets often. They wrote them on typewriters, copied them and spread them by hand. So soon typewriters had to be registered, typefaces checked. She was in a 'safe' house because of my father. She went to secret readings of poetry – no, not Yevtushenko, I think, but others. Many years later she told me I was conceived after she returned from a secret meeting in 1971 where she heard the BBC broadcasting *samizdat* that had been smuggled abroad. Then the broadcasts were – yes, 'jammed', you say, yes?

What about me? I was born in 1971 – they could not afford a child before. I left biology for English and tourism. It is a hard school. We have to learn everything by rote. Yes, I do repeat words they tell us to – when we are afraid of forgetting what comes next. Or just thinking. My friends and I do not go to the *dacha*. We like discos and music. Yes, I think I prefer life after *perestroika*. We believed capitalism must be better than what we had. Now I do not know. We have the freedom you talk so much about but nowhere to go and nothing to do with our lives. Few jobs, no security, no future. Before, we were not allowed to leave Russia; now we can leave for anywhere in the world, but your country and others do not welcome us. The requirements for a visa are impossible. Before imprisoned by Russia; now by the world. It comes to the same.

We are told that Nicholas II will be proclaimed a martyr just because he had a violent death, like Paul I, the first of the Romanovs. Yes, as you say, it is 'neat symmetry', but I am not sure whether it means anything for the people. Neat symmetry, in history, is probably right. Many like my mother see him as a murderer. As she had to learn Stalin was, though she believed in him for so long. For a great cause, she was told, a purge helped the workers to a greater future. Nicholas II and Stalin signed away the lives of thousands or millions of us Russians. To help our future. Or our country, if that is not the same?

The Russian people defeat Napoleon, Hitler, enemies from without. Our heroes turn into enemies from within. It is our fate.

So the last of the Romanovs are home in Saint Petersburg, 80 years late, without the Tsarevich of the same name as Peter the Great's son, Alexei, murdered as I told you, by his father in this fortress. More neat symmetry still. The poor ill Tsarevich Alexei's bones are missing, like his sister Maria's. More unquiet souls. So too Lenin. Some time our present 'holy fool' may send Lenin back to his mother's side. A humbler funeral, I think, in the city once named after him. More neat historical symmetry.

The empty red granite mausoleum in Moscow? What will happen to it? I think it will stay and Lenin will join Stalin and the other statues standing guard behind it. It will stay vacant, as Russia's ultimate monument to empty dreams. No more heroes.

You told me that Stalin's daughter not long ago said to someone in the West that the only way to cure our illness is to kill 20,000 more Russians. Like father, like daughter; massacres from within. Will it ever change? I do not want to feel part of the tide of history: centuries of Tsars, then Lenin, Stalin, capitalism – what is their legacy? When I was a little girl, I looked at the horizon and saw *babushka*'s blossom and rowan berries. Now, after *glasnost* and the coming of freedom, I only see snow and fog. How we remember history shapes our hopes. All I dream of now is food, shelter, a chance to think out a life. To love perhaps?

I am so confused.

I just want to sit down by the Neva and weep.

*The Winter Palace
and the
River Neva*

*Peter and Paul
Cathedral*

⌘

for Robert

⌘

THE BEST YEARS

I was one of the 'Mrs. Thatcher, milk snatcher' kids, deprived from the start, at least as far as my schooldays went. My mother's anxiety was felt from those infant years; perched in the child's bicycle seat behind her, I was whisked around and suffered from her being accident-prone. I have become familiar with the inside of hospitals from an early age, unwillingly of course, such as when I was unpinned from beneath a security van. It was just one of those countless occasions when her reasoning went wobbly. Think of a wide garage forecourt, the office straight ahead, and the security van in front of it. We were going to swoop across to pay for the car repairs, sling the decrepit bicycle into the boot of our elderly estate car, and save time by returning home before the rush hour. In the event we lost the whole evening, nearly a whole night. She had been taught to give a wide berth to horses' hooves due to their tendency to kick, so she swooped round the rear of the van as it began to back out, pinning her under the bicycle and me under the vehicle. She went hysterical over me although she suffered the worst cuts and scrapes. I was unharmed though scared. As I said, it was the first of many incidents when, to save time, we lost bags of it. My parents were always saying that the road to Hell is paved with good intentions. I sincerely fear for them.

It was a world of smells: oil under that van, the worn leather of the bicycle saddle and the washing-machine soap mingled oddly with hints of my mother's last foray into perfume drifting from her much worn navy-blue jacket. Worst of all were the burnt vegetables, cabbage especially, rising vertically to reach my den on the top floor and mysteriously by-passing my mother's study, where she was engrossed in preparing her latest class. She couldn't bear to wait around in the kitchen,

'Potatoes take ages to cook. Think what I could get done in twenty minutes!'

'Mummy, something's burning!' I won't repeat her language, but I am willing to bet no other household has thrown away more burnt saucepans.

I could never make out whether my father played at being absent-minded, or really was. This speculation I shared with my mother, who found his vagueness highly provocative. To me it could serve as a shield. Take my music education. Both my parents were keen for me to have one, but my mother delegated this responsibility to him. Fatal. I could overhear them discussing which instrument they might propose to me, as I didn't show any particular propensity for the piano, violin or cello all lying around in the house. They decided on a cornet, as a way of catering for what they called 'my hyperactive tendencies'. My father would find a moment more to his liking than mine, place a piece to practise on a music stand in front of me, then disappear down the narrow stairs from my den. I quit as soon as he was out of earshot.

They both decided it was a waste of time to continue when, a year or so later, I left my cornet on Derby station – by mistake, of course – while returning from visiting Granny. I did learn how to read music, and that at least I can thank my father for. As for the cornet, I hardly played more than a couple of bars each practice time, just to accompany his departing advice.

You may wonder how I knew what my parents were brewing up for me. They first spoke in French and didn't bother about my being in earshot until they suspected, after I'd taken French for one year, that I might be able to follow the gist. The habit really lapsed because my father's school French had retired so gracefully many, many years ago that he was hardly up to it. My mother's angry frustration led her to give up on him. But they still underestimated my hearing capacity, helped by the way they tended to discuss things some distance away from each other. I was amused by the odd conclusions they came to. When in my second year at secondary school I had to take either or both French and German, I chose German without saying a word to them. They only discovered when it was too late; it wasn't their decision or their life, anyway. My mother immediately concluded that it was a sign of teenage rebellion; she could help me with French, but knew no German. Nothing of the sort. The German teacher was marginally less hopeless than the French one. However, of this I didn't disabuse her.

Before their headlong battles with the Department of Education, our language teachers arranged visits, and I went on one to Cologne. Or it was to be, but for some reason we were switched to Hamburg at the last minute. We set off before Easter for an overnight coach journey to the Channel port. I can still see my mother there, fondly waving me goodbye while still holding my ration of sandwiches, drink and pocket money in the other hand. I was prevented from starving through scraps of food and some liquid offered by the others. She's always planning, my mum, but sometimes overdoes it and things just don't work out the way they should.

Perhaps she is the absent-minded one? Better not tell her.

I forgot to mention the discussions which I don't think I was supposed to hear concerning which secondary school to send me to. They finally decided on one positioned neatly on my father's way to work which was single sex, because of the silly idea that girls distract boys, never vice versa which would be nearer the truth. Anyway, there was no fear of distraction from the specimens I used to see scratching around our local girls-only establishment, believe me!

Don't tell me about *Tom Brown's Schooldays* because I went through it all. I didn't like to mention it at the time, because all the other boys in my year were shooting up, voices breaking and wisps of beard appearing. I may have been among the youngest in the year, but my adulthood was slow in coming. The worst thing about it was my mother's concern. It sort of enveloped me. I didn't tell anyone about the bullying at first, and worked out ways of avoiding the two who picked on me. One lived in a road I always took on the way home. It all came out when a note was pushed through the door with threats and demands for money. My mother picked it up – something they should have realised was more than likely. She always wanted to 'talk things through' with me, part of my growing-up education, I sensed. 'Bullies are rarely the ones who do best at school. They're usually large physically, but with little self-confidence.' I suppose she was right. Neither did well in class, and one had a father in and out of prison, so I gather he had his reasons for getting at me. I agreed to go to the headmaster to talk it over, and he sorted it out. Still, not one of my most pleasant 'educational' experiences.

One of the reasons I wanted to go to this school was because it had so many after-school clubs. In my first year I joined ones for table tennis and chess. It was great. We stayed on after school and had fun with teachers. Then it was all stopped, and the battle with Thatcher's government droned on for most of my years at school. All that fun and goodwill, a sort of tradition I imagine, withered away. Will it ever return? More real education went on then, I think, than in the classroom.

Mother seemed to expect me to be in the top set for everything. That would never be the case, and I did warn her. I seemed to do best in the subjects which were, in theory, taught individually in mixed ability groups. They were English and history, and what with the dinner table talk at home – admittedly with everyone piping up at the same time – and the books all over the place, I didn't expect problems. But in the selected groups I was always anchored to the middle, or just below, the top group. My mother's efforts redoubled. No chance to see the teachers except through individual requests and in school hours, as the long war with government directives meant the teachers were on an outside-school-hours-activities strike. For four years there were no parent-teacher meetings, causing my mother to froth at the mouth.

She had an on-going battle with my social life, such as it was. As she had always done in her family, she insisted on having family dinner at 7.30 in the evening. Now, by seven, my friends had finished their tea, and were knocking at the door. She had me send them upstairs and put the dinner time forward to seven, but NO earlier.

'We're not hungry at six,' my father complained, 'and then, if I eat early, I'm only famished again by ten.' My parents never went to bed before midnight, so I suppose they had a point. I was miffed at not being able to watch TV programmes between seven and eight during the sacred dinner hour, and did once try to slither out with my plate. I was caught, and a few days later I found a video recorder tucked under the TV set with a packet of blank video tapes.

'For you, Mark,' my mother told me. 'You can record anything you like on them.' I knew they reserved the right to take sneaked looks at my TV fodder. No matter. Nothing said, all understood.

My verbal education was nurtured with my body at these dinner sessions, to provoke them both to grow. Parental rules allowed no more than five minutes on football or sport with my brothers and a maximum of five minutes on food. No criticism of the menu of 'healthy' brown bread and salads was allowed, as mother threatened she would go on strike. The rest of us caved in promptly. She would have been capable . . . We nearly reached the brink many times, but didn't quite tip over, mainly thanks to Father's moderation. He's good at picking up danger signs early on before they became deadly. But it has turned me now into a MacDonald's junkie.

So we would chew over books, the arts, politics – that's how I found out I was a 'Thatcher child', got keen on films, and discussed on a daily basis all manner of things but sport and food. We were an argumentative lot, but my parents made sure there were subjects galore to discuss and digest. Mother further pursued my education with cuttings from the newspapers she read.

'How on earth did you know that, Mark?' She would ask, ever curious.

'From a cutting you gave me to read, Mummy!'

'Oh!' with a pleasant mixture of embarrassment and satisfaction. Something was penetrating my numbskull, though not much of it manifested itself in good marks. I bumbled along, doing just well enough not to cause major concern. Except to her.

Dad found me the pool table. How we got it up the narrow stairs and pigmy-sized door to my den I don't know. It must have grown with me, as it could never retreat its way out, so the room is forever to be swamped by the green baize sward which my mother was convinced became the cause of my less than brilliant school achievements. She never got over her apprehension at the sight of a large patch of green.

I liked doing things, painting lots of toy soldiers or making model planes, ships, or, presents from my father, buildings. I even started collections of all sorts, and had numerous little places to put my interesting bits and pieces. I even set to building more shelves to display all my models. The planes hung from beams and scared my parents when they came into the room in the dark. It was a time of bliss when I bought two or more models a week and was the envy of my friends. There was a model shop in the next road but one, and I was in there most days. If he hadn't got it in stock, Jim, the proprietor, would look at catalogues and choose more complicated models for me to get stuck into.

'Who's Jim?' my mother asked one Saturday morning as I was settling down to the model I had ordered earlier in the week.

'He's the model shop man.'

'Which model shop man? Does he make them?'

'No. Sells.' I wished she would go away so I could concentrate. This was part of my learning curve, and I needed to work on it without having her hanging over me. But no, on she went, 'He says you owe him money . . . '

That was the end of a long and lovely relationship. She went out that afternoon, paid the £40 on my account, and forbade him to sell me anything that wasn't for cash. I bargained for more pocket money and did get a rise, but that signalled the end of my great modelling days. I was still given big and complicated ones for Christmas and birthday, but never had that cosy sort of relationship with Jim again. Sad, but there you go!

He shut up shop a year or so later, and that put paid to my model-making career.

35

At that time – I was about 14 – I was having fun in our local town. I was allowed out on my own, as long as I said where I was going and who with.

One evening my father said, 'Who's Harry?' I felt sort of proud at being able to mention adults by first name like that. It followed on from the satisfaction of shocking the parents when I was learning to string together long sentences and enjoying my first experience of language power. 'Knickers' or some other mildly unmentionable word for a child of four would create the required shock horror, and now, with more than a dollop of admiration from others, I referred to adults with familiarity – me, just a teenager!

'Harry has a shop down the High Street.' My mother looked up, her ears pricking frantically. I knew what she wanted to hear. 'He sells toys, mostly for young children, and is great fun. So's his wife. We just talk a lot. He's brilliant.'

'I thought that shop sold cigarettes?' Mother has never been good at supposedly innocent questions.

'Not now. Sweets.' So Harry was one of my stops along the local High Street which buzzed with thrills and temptations.

One night I was picked up by a bobby on a bicycle. I was furious. My mother always said she would phone the police if I hadn't returned by eleven and she didn't know where I was. She must have been fantasising about teenage paperboys who are assaulted and murdered. Anyway, I had told her where I was going that night, but it happened I left one friend to accompany another back home. She told me how worried she was to find I wasn't where I said I would be. I had left some time before, so the commiseration from my friend's mother rubbed her up entirely the wrong way. I was picked up while cycling back home just after 11.30. My mother had to learn to be patient and a bit more flexible. At the sight of my face she only had time to read half the riot act. The matter was never referred to again.

By this time I was on the brink of becoming a national guinea-pig for new exams, so every kid could escape from obligatory education with 'something to show for it'. O for Ordinary levels were dead, long live the GCSE, or 'General Certificate for School Ediots', as the ensuing confusion suggested. The 'ediots' were a new breed of educational idiots setting assessment tests where cheating, or ghost writing and the chance to earn a bit of money on the side, flourished. About the same time all my friends were given sport video games, and the 'curse of the green baize', as she would have it, reappeared.

'Not baize, Mummy. It's supposed to be grass . . .' I became the unacknowledged champion of these football games, and each evening sneaked down to our set, or out to my friends', when my parents thought I was studying. I upset my father by informing him I had no intention of becoming a 'swot', as he would put it, and he thought I was referring to him. Strained times.

I dreaded the peace treaty between Thatcher's minions and the teachers' union because parent-teacher meetings were on the agenda again. We had one just before our crucial GCSEs. The place was packed with worried parents, some accompanied by their offspring. I naturally refused to attend this scene of acute embarrassment, to see my mother bearing down on some hapless teacher, such as the physics one who announced that I might think more clearly if my work were more tidily presented.

'Are you sure you are referring to my son?' He assured her he was.

'If anything, Mark's work is more presentational than substantial . . .' He must have been relieved to see the back of her. One science teacher, Mr. Hornby, who was a nice, caring sort of person, did take time to praise me, and later steered me through the Science Sixth. I could never understand at the time why my mother blew a chill air on all he said about me. She divulged nothing, just pursed her lips and changed the subject. That was ominous.

Things changed after that meeting. No more inveighing against the 'green baize', or calling up the narrow staircase, 'Are you studying? I can hear you playing pool.' Instead, from the very same vantage point, she occasionally called out, 'How are you getting on, Mark? My duty is to warn you that these exams will shape your future life. But it's your life, not mine. You must decide.'

My parents were never ones to parade their children's academic successes like trophies before their admiring or envious friends, so my string of Bs and a couple of Cs did not dismay them unduly. Most of their friends' children were vying to out-do the As of their peers. I had just one, unexpectedly, in a science subject I was never supposed to shine at. Mr. Hornby's speciality.

So it was that I chose it and a strait-laced group of related subjects as decreed by the university entrance requirements at the time. Out went my beloved history and English – I had just read the minimum for them, but got my Bs painlessly, so I should have continued. Sadly it was not to be. Mr. Hornby began to loom large in my life, and my mother's incomprehensible agitation was felt. I had to find out what was behind it all, but for some reason she didn't want to tell me. Then, through some chance remark I learnt that Mr. Hornby, my teacher at the time, had been given my IQ tests done at the end of primary school. During the last of the parent-teacher meetings when, aged 11, I had arrived at the secondary school and before the boycott of such events, Mr. Hornby had told my parents, tactlessly, my score was low and that I would probably be unable to keep them company intellectually. My father had neatly forgotten such a dire prognostication, but it nagged on in my mother's mind for many a long year, it seems. Stranger than fiction, here was that very same assessor of my low IQ status steering me firmly towards university and my future career!

Providence was working overtime at this point, or why else would I have met Dr. Featherstone? He had been a rather distant figure teaching some specialised aspect of science at our local university and figuring on our school's Board of Governors. He then offered, as he had done for many years, to tutor those of us thinking of specialising in his field, and even coaching at his home the small group attempting scholarship level. Nurtured benignly by Mr. Hornby at school, we were gently urged to make our way out of town to Dr. Featherstone's house and spend an evening a week with him. My cycle was crammed into the back of a newer estate car, and I was deposited at the end of his drive. I really enjoyed those evenings, with study, talk, coffee and biscuits, before speeding home downhill all the way.

We all passed, thanks to Dr. Featherstone in particular, rather well.

As my undergraduate years sped by, my mother started up again. 'Remember, a little sprinkling of appreciation from a young person means so very much to the older generation. Don't forget what Dr. Featherstone has done for you. See him, and keep him up to date with what you're doing. Also Mr. Hornby.'

Time passed, but I usually did drop in at the staff room when home, and drove out to see Dr. Featherstone, busy as ever. He was particularly pleased when I sent him my first publication, my name among many others, but, as he pointed out with 'let's celebrate' generosity, 'it's an important start, Mark'. His smile was as huge as ever, but he had begun to look a bit frail. Strange, because he can't have been more than in his mid-fifties. Right then I determined to dedicate my first substantial paper to him. 'Dr. Featherstone has cancer,' my father told me over the phone. 'Do send him the piece you're dedicating to him.' I felt I was being bossed around. I had published a number of pieces since the first, none substantial enough to merit a dedication to someone who, after all, had moulded my future. It had to be something extra special. I knew what I was doing, thank you very much!

About a year later on my way home for a short visit, I bumped into our local vicar on the train. He warned me there had been changes at school. Most of the staff I knew had left or taken early retirement. He doubted I would recognise anyone in the staff room now. That put me off a bit. I did look in while passing, and had a few words with my former English teacher. Mr. Hornby had gone, and most of the other good teachers. The older lot, the more experienced, had been pensioned off early. I felt too depressed to see Dr. Featherstone, and my mother's insistence I should find time, because he was ill and so on, just got my back up. Jim's old model shop was now a thriving unisex hairdresser's! Harry was still there, ever welcoming. I reported back, to my parents' satisfaction, that he had phased out tobacco completely. Mother hinted that she wouldn't have much reason to buy anything from his shop until she had grandchildren, which I didn't, of course, hear.

A month or so later I did actually finish the first important paper I had researched and written on my own, and had it accepted for a key journal in my field. This would be worthy of Dr. Featherstone. I asked advice and composed a suitable dedication – though not too fulsome, as he would be disconcerted. But it did show how much I owed to him and it would cheer him up.

The off-prints took a few weeks to arrive. I was slipping his into an envelope with a brief note, and writing his address when the phone rang.

I am not given to crying. It's not that I don't feel distress, but it tends to make me gruff and angry as a sort of self-defence. At the thought of what happened a sort of desolation spreads over me, and then the nagging remorse at the sadness of it all.

My mother had rung to tell me Dr. Featherstone had died the previous week.

for Pat and Eric

'THE PURSUIT OF HAPPINESS'

Excitement was tempered by anxiety. This much filmed, painted, written and talked-about city of New York looked just as Louise expected when the jet from London descended into Kennedy Airport. The familiar skyscrapers pierced the skyline as the yellow shark taxi took her in through Queens. The World Trade Center was higher than the Empire State Building, though not so elegant, her driver observed, but the Chrysler Building beat all others for style . . . He sensed it was her first visit to New York. But, once inside the Manhattan grid, she began to make her own discoveries. The streets were wider, the skyscrapers more spaced out; some of the more resilient older houses surviving cheek by jowl with their bossier neighbours. The taxi stopped outside a brownstone.

It had only five floors but boasted all the conveniences of a Manhattan skyscraper – a lift, behind it a dumbwaiter, both starting from the basement and heading up to the roof garden. Mutual friends had suggested to Louise Williamson that she should stay with some distant relatives who were open-hearted and centrally placed. It would be confusing, they advised, if not downright dangerous, for her to unravel the express and local trains on the subway system, which would be inevitable were she to find quarters in Brooklyn or the Bronx. She had only been married for a few months when unexpectedly she was invited to work on an exhibition of rare manuscripts, to be shown both in New York and London; it involved at least one month's research at the Pierpont Morgan Library in Manhattan.

Elizabeth Daneman, flanked by her two small dogs, was there in the hall to welcome her. The walls were hung with paintings on bark, strange instruments and wide-brimmed hats with patterns in red or green, earth tones. Unexpected niches in a wall or on the stairs lit from behind finely-woven baskets and strange figures, their forms still rough from the hands that had created them out of primeval clay.

'Dan's collection of the best he can find or afford in Mexico.' Elizabeth anticipated Louise's question, kindly avoiding her any embarrassing show of ignorance. The trouble was that, because she had studied illuminated manuscripts, it was assumed she was expert in all aspects of art history and knew far more than she did. It provoked in her an air of anxiety which was not immediately appealing.

'Please call me Liz,' her hostess requested as they stepped out of the lift on the fourth floor and into a light blue and green room with a potted palm in one corner. 'Everyone else does.'

It was sunny, the air crisp. White blossom was struggling out into early April. She saw she was in the shadow line of a twenty-floor skyscraper next door. It darkened the projecting bay window of her room, while the sun shone straight into the windows opposite, illuminating the innumerable floors of a square-windowed characterless apartment block. It was like looking into so many stills of a 1930s film of domestic life. She turned away, feeling intrusive, and busied herself hanging clothes in the ample wall cupboard, arranging her toiletries around the original 1920s bathroom fittings of light blue tiles edged with the thinnest of green lines. It was a sky and foliage colour combination, she mused, as she laid out her notes and prepared for her first visit to the Library. She was to meet the curators there in two days' time; she could catch up on sleep by going to bed early and not setting the alarm. All had been minutely planned, hour by hour, before she boarded the plane.

The telephone rang, startling her. Green on a green side-table, it continued ringing and a red light went on and off rhythmically. Should she answer it? She lifted the receiver and ventured, 'Hello, it's Louise.'

'Oh good, I forgot to explain the phone to you and all the other idiosyncrasies of this house. Would you like to come down for supper? We could have an early one together as you must be tired.'

What a relief. She would have to explore the shops and change some money the next day. Liz, with her immaculately manicured hands and hair – blond, swept back and upwards with chic assurance – daunted her. She wore a clean-cut clear blue suit on a body conspicuously firm and compact. Louise was already casting herself in a new role as the country mouse; Liz, in contrast, was the slightly threatening epitome of city sophistication.

Hot watercress soup, croutons, delicious brown bread with strange tastes kneaded into it, and fresh fruit salad, all with iced tea, was the sum total of supper. It would not have appeased Louise's normally heartier appetite, were it not for the first wave of jet lag warning her that sleep was the first and only required nourishment at this juncture. She beamed her thanks and hastened to help stack the dishwasher so she could learn her way around the house and not be a burden on her hosts. Liz could not have been more helpful, with an informality that was belied by her appearance.

Louise sank into heavy slumber, disrupted only by the sound of sirens. Her room faced the street; even with windows sealed, the city's fretting night sounds communicated a sense of unease. Lucky she had set aside the next day to find her bearings, make sure she knew how to get to the museums, and the Pierpont Morgan Library in particular. She woke with a muzzy head in some consternation. A car alarm was screeching at the end of the street. Sleep defeated, she went to take a shower, and by the time she returned to the bedroom, it had stopped. That was a relief, but somehow the day had started out of kilter. It was still only 4 am in New York.

She was welcomed to English muffins at the breakfast table by Dan, a cheerful early riser who went jogging in Central Park every morning, whatever the weather. She learnt he had started his collection of artefacts from Mexico on his frequent trips there, 'for business and pleasure' as he neatly put it. He enjoyed the informality it gave to his otherwise over-structured life working in a Wall Street firm. Their children were living independent lives, as yet unmarried. Liz was nowhere to be seen. Was she out already, or a late riser as Louise normally was? It would be prying for her to find out, so instead she enquired where the nearest food shops were, and was told of a market two streets east and then one block downtown. So rational, this city's layout.

If anyone could get lost in a simple grid street system, then it was Louise. It was easy to find the bank Dan had indicated on Third Avenue, only one block east from her own street. She had remembered to bring her passport, so there was no problem changing a traveller's cheque. So far so good. Now to cross another cavernous avenue, then turn one block uptown. This she did, veering left. One block passed. No market at all. She could hardly have missed the hubbub of market stalls. Another block. No, the shops were for every sort of inedible product from clothes to candles and antiques. Not the right area, she supposed, for a scruffy food market. Five blocks later it dawned on her that this might be the wrong direction. She retraced her steps and went uphill, beyond the intersection with 62nd street. Still uphill, so how could the direction be 'downtown'? Strangely illogical in a rational grid system. Still no market, only a food shop in the first block on the left, with hardly room to push the small versions of the usual supermarket trolleys up and down the stacks crammed full of every imaginable variety. She searched for coffee, and here it was stacked in large sizes of regular, decaffeinated, perfumed or flavoured in countless ways. The bread varieties were even more confusing. She tried to decipher what she wanted from the ingredients, deciding to avoid the many varieties with sugar – strange, that was. Bread, sugar. Muffins, not just the plain 'English' variety, but stacks of them in all shapes and sizes containing anything from the obvious raisins to cranberries, bananas or even squash – what on earth was that? She seemed to recall some sort of 'squash' bread – Liz would explain.

The subway trains were easier. The next day, Louise's first at the Library, she followed Liz's instructions, deftly slipping a token into the turnstile, and scurried down the side marked 'downtown'. 'Uptown' on her return. Not hard at all, and this was only her second journey! She felt quite at ease, alert again inside the Big Apple. Fleeting figures passed by, bustling up or down or across the street and avenue grid pattern; all seemed briskly, energetically busy. Inside the Library the atmosphere was pleasant and brisk too. Everyone seemed to have an endless string of tasks to be completed cheerfully and efficiently in the shortest time possible. She spent a useful but rather breathless half-hour with the curator of rare manuscripts and left excited about her forthcoming exhibition.

Home again, safe and sound, she let herself in. Lights were on in the hall and kitchen, but the place seemed deserted. She poured herself a glass of orange juice and sat down by the working surface along one side of the kitchen to gather up her thoughts and energies. Her eyes strayed over the fruit, pen and bits of paper with messages just in case someone wanted to see her, and were drawn to what seemed to be a child's attempt at hieroglyphics. A few letters, then a shape or mini drawing, followed by a number. Strangely intrigued by it, Louise averted her eyes for no other reason than embarrassment at being caught reading, or trying to decipher, a message or perhaps messages not meant for her. Had she stumbled upon a hidden agenda?

'How did your first day go?' Louise jumped and turned to see Liz at the door. She must have been to the hairdresser's; her hair was so immaculate, gleamingly blonde, set off by a cool green dress and jacket outfit of heavy silk. 'Forgive us if we go to the opera tonight. We have subscription tickets with friends. The day after tomorrow we are planning a dinner party here and hope you can join us.'

Of course she could. Apart from her duties at the Library, she had no fixed plans. She had no friends in New York, and soon found out that her new colleagues were all doing evening courses and studying for yet more diplomas or even doctorates. Little time to spare for socialising.

Two days later she returned at midday. A strange man was seated bent over the kitchen working surface, smoking and phoning. She paused in the doorway. He seemed too familiar with the set-up to be an intruder. The telephone conversation finished with a flourish, he glanced up, and –

'I'm Carl. Are you our guest from England?'

'Yes. Louise Williamson.'

He twisted out his cigarette in an ashtray, scanning her as he did it, then turned to a plate supporting a mega-sandwich, like a skyscraper rising from a foundation of speckled brown bread through storeys of Liz's chicken, leftover from the previous day. It was loosely constructed with gherkins and splodges of mayonnaise, both from opened bottles crammed into the fridge, crisp lemon-green lettuce leaves brightly interfurled with neatly-sliced tomatoes, all topped by a light slice of white bread with caraway seeds.

'I'll make you one?' Carl offered generously. 'I think there is still some chicken lying around.'

'No. Thanks – I really appreciate it, but I'm not very hungry.' Louise wasn't attracted by the prospect of forcing her jaws open wide enough to bite into such a generous offering of squashy ingredients. Carl watched her spread some butter onto a couple of slices of caraway seed bread, balance some wedges of leftover Brie on it, and arrange a few bits of lettuce and tomatoes on a separate plate.

'Not hungry?' He looked at her with pity. 'Where have you been?'

'Just to the Library where I'm working for a month,' she said after finishing a mouthful. ' This afternoon I plan to go to Washington Square. I want to see what's left of the area Henry James wrote about.'

'Have you been to the Village?' he asked.

'Greenwich Village?'

Carl nodded, his face lighting up. 'Yes, that's my favourite haunt.'

'Well, sort of. All I could find were streets of warehouses converted into one art gallery after another. They were quite interesting, but some of the art was way out, sort of installation stuff where you went inside and found rags and bits of sculpture and dolls and toys all hanging from the hidden ceiling high in the darkness above, and it reminded me of the ghost train in fairs when I . . . ' her voice trailed into silence as Carl got up while she was speaking, cleared his plate and cutlery away, and said he had to get on. There was a lot to do before the dinner party. Louise nodded, and allowed herself to take the lift, though the four-floor climb up the stairs was supposed to get her into trim. She needed to indulge herself a bit, she thought. She had promised herself she would write a diary, and now she had a moment to get it up to date, before going to see Washington Square. Instead of a description of the Pierpont Morgan Library, she started with one of Carl.

Still jet-lagged, Louise fell asleep before words had descended onto the second page. She needed a cup of tea to wake her up four hours later. Down in the kitchen Carl's tall lean figure was inclined over a large and elaborate flower arrangement. She paused to admire it, and the gaze of his liquid, slightly round brown eyes seemed to invite her into his thoughts.

'I still need to shop for this evening. The flowers I bought on the way here, also the wine. They'll deliver that. I still need to get the food. Would you help me?

Washington Square could wait for another day. She felt instead that she could get a better sense of the city by going with Carl, and, anyway, shopping was hardly intellectually demanding. She wanted some mental relief, she decided.

'Yes. When?'

'When you're ready.'

They set off with Carl giving a running commentary on the shops they passed. One 'market' as he called it, meaning a supermarket, or a food store, was good but very pricey. This fruit and vegetable shop – they both stopped to peer into the colourful emporium – was the best for fresh supplies and had everything ready washed, so that saved a lot of time. The Daneman household did most of their buying at the same store she had been to on her first day in the city. It was adequate, and best value. Louise was pleased he was using Liz's money in the most economical way, while not cutting down on quality for her dinner party. He took her to the now familiar stacks:

'The make she likes is red, somewhere down there. Can you tell me what it's called?'

'Buitoni.' Why doesn't he put on his glasses like me to read the labels, Louise thought, piqued. Carl inspected the shapes inside.

'That's right. Another, but green.' So it would be a mixed colour cold pasta salad, perhaps? She rather enjoyed this undemanding detective work. On to another stack.

'When twelve or so people are coming, I always tell Mrs. Daneman to serve one sort of coffee and say decaff. I think it's blue.' Again the blue labels were piled near the ground. Louise bent down to check the label. He was right. Decaffeinated coffee.

'The largest.' He saw her hesitating. And so they continued. By the end of the excursion her back was aching as everything he needed seemed to be near floor level. At least they had nothing to carry. It would all be delivered. Nor did he have to pay. Liz had an account. It all took about half the time she expected, and they were shopping for twelve people!

On their return there was joyful barking from Alpha and Beta, two small plump dogs aspiring to be fox terriers, half sisters as their fathers had muddied the pure descent from their pedigree mother, Stasia. Liz had bought Stasia fifteen years earlier, partly to deter burglars, partly to breed, but found she enjoyed her intelligent company more than the hassle with puppies and breeders' certificates. However, Stasia had escaped and produced two litters; Liz decided to keep one from each, to continue the line. They were too far down for Carl to bend his six-foot-four frame, but he adeptly tipped his left shoe up between their front legs and tickled them in turn. They followed him everywhere in silent adoration, but only when Liz was out.

It seemed to be assumed by Carl that Louise would help with the preparations: carrying the flowers to strategic positions in the dining-room on the ground floor; pulling silver down from the first and second floors in the dumb waiter, the first time she had ever worked such a useful device. Glasses, soda water, tonic, bitter lemon, whisky, and bourbon, she placed them through one hatch into the dumb waiter; then on its return journey she put in nuts, tortilla-flavoured chips, and dips prepared for them, to be retrieved through the hatch in the serving room off the first-floor sitting room. Up and down went the dumb waiter with bewildering regularity for an hour. Finally Carl told her he wanted to concentrate on laying the table and decorating the first dish, which would be a very special salad placed at each setting. Salad for starters, not as a side dish for the main course. How strange, Louise thought, how inventive – perhaps? Salad on its own never seemed particularly appetising to her. It was one of those dishes that went with something else, which sort of set it off. Never mind.

'Go and get ready,' advised Carl. 'Women always need twice the time,' he added with what she heard as a titter. Louise looked at him, almost frowning.

'Like this.' Carl put down the dishes he was about to carry to the table and mimicked a woman plucking her eyebrows, patting cream on her face, arranging eye shadow, while eyeing her all the time and shifting his weight from one leg to the other, knee-crossing in between in the stereotyped female model position. Initially Louise felt indignant, but, reckoning the performance must have been polished by a number of previous presentations, she resolved not to give him satisfaction. Instead, she just smiled as if nothing in particular had happened,

'Sorry, Carl, you're going to be disappointed when I tell you that I don't have the time, or inclination as it happens, for such activities. Not that sort. A shame?'

He looked at her, pursed his lips, but, before he could slip in a deft, maybe cutting comment, she added, 'And I'm sure you'd say it shows!' She turned on her heels, taking out with her his look of thwarted astonishment as she determined to run up the stairs this time to her retreat on the fourth floor.

Dinner parties assume various flavours. This one her palate anticipated as easy going yet stimulatingly strange. The guests assembled in the magnificent sombre first-floor sitting room, panelled and topped by a carved oak ceiling from the baronial hall of some forgotten Scottish castle, installed many years before the Danemans moved in. She was introduced to so many people that, the moment uttered, their names slid off her memory. Sitting nervously on the edge of her chair, Louise tried to balance her drink while attempting to poke the chips into the drippy, tasty dips she had placed there herself. Carl was in the background dispensing drinks for Dan, who conveyed them to the guests, chatting all the time about the Mexican collection, occasionally giving a wary answer to some query about movements on Wall Street. Louise admired the way he steered clear of business and on to what he clearly considered more interesting topics. Liz introduced Louise as an expert on manuscripts, and she immediately became the centre of a circle of admiration.

'Louise's been invited to do research at the Pierpont Morgan Library,' Dan announced to all and sundry. Murmurs of approval all round.

'I should like to talk to you about the exhibition you're working on,' said one of the guests, a tall slender dealer friend of Liz's with a commanding voice and the warmest smile imaginable. 'I'd be delighted if you could come and see my own manuscript collection. Perhaps you could give me some advice?' Carl appeared briefly at the top of the stairs and beckoned to Liz. It was time to eat.

The deep green mixed lettuce salad with Gorgonzola cheese diced over it, and what looked like soup croutons too, was topped by little light green curls which turned out to be avocado. There was plenty of iced water and white wine. Red wine followed, raising the tone of the conversation as Dan disappeared into the pantry to carve. The culinary masterpiece appeared on a huge oval platter: this must have been Carl's secret *tour de force*, a roasted leg of lamb in a nest of two-tone pasta supporting vegetables of all seasons, from baby maize to mange tout, red, green, yellow peppers, courgettes, you name it, it was there. Had Carl prepared all this after Louise had been 'dismissed'? That would have been less than two hours before the first guests arrived. Or was it the result of his orchestration of pre-cooked foods, heated in the microwave to appear hot and tasty in unison?

The beguiling simplicity of the three-sorbet desert of strawberry, white vanilla and blue cranberry provided a welcome contrast; Louise was so impressed at the subtle way her hosts had chosen to make her feel at home. Red, white and blue, the colours of the Union Jack. She beamed, and found others were also responding, but not in any way connected with her presence. Then she noticed a tiny flag in the same three colours with stars and stripes discreetly tucked into the centre of the softening mounds of sorbet.

'The red, white and blue!' said her neighbour, a musician with a large white moustache and genial smile.

'Oh, I thought they were the colours of the French flag?' replied Louise with what she hoped was an air of innocence. But he had turned away and probably didn't hear.

The lady with the antique dealing business was shocking the company at dessert over the illiteracy crisis in the USA.

'I support the nation-wide campaign because I want to give something back to society.' She smiled at her husband down the far end of the table. 'I don't take my good fortune in meeting such a wonderful man as my husband lightly, you know,' making him turn beetroot and look desperately at his Harvard friend, Dan, to rescue him. 'So I want to give something back,' she reiterated, oblivious. '40,000,000 people in the USA can barely read or write!'

Louise stared at her unbelievingly from the other side of the dinner table. With all the stress on education, all those schools, colleges, universities, her colleagues, the whole country seemed to be in the process of retraining for something, and yet . . .

'Immigrants, I suppose. Especially from Latin America, perhaps?' she asked, remembering all the Spanish speakers she had heard in the subway. But nearly one sixth of a nation – no, not possible.

'No. Many have been here for generations. Whites. Ones who have fallen through the system. If found out, they can't drive. They are a danger to everyone else because they can't read the notices. We have schemes, one-to-one teaching, so they can have more of a chance, and their families too. We must, must let them free. I feel so passionately about this. They need help badly. Now.'

Carl, still keeping in the background, had closed the dining-room door into the hall for some reason. Nobody noticed, except Liz and Louise.

'Alpha probably had an accident and he's dealing with it,' Liz explained quietly. 'We could hardly have everyone paddling out through it! Marble floors are so easy to mop. Lucky it happened before the Cinderella hour!'

There was no sign of Carl before or after the guests left at about eleven. Louise looked bemused.

'Carl never stays on after 10.30, and even that's a special favour he says he only does for me,' Liz explained, 'and only if he is paid extra by 10 o'clock. He lays down his conditions!'

The kitchen was immaculate. Louise did not dare ask whether he had cooked the main dish. Liz was on the phone to her son in Minneapolis; Dan retired to his library next to the sitting-room on the first floor, and Louise to her room and the diary.

Carl was not seen or heard from for four days.

The literacy lady's words echoed through Louise's mind for days on end. Education as a passport to freedom. Sounds good. Sounds right. These thoughts were still puzzling her one sunny afternoon when she felt the urge to go and survey the joggers, roller skaters and cyclists in Central Park. She marvelled at the maelstrom of energy these New Yorkers channelled into making money, jogging, the enjoyment of zealously nurtured health, culture, family life and friends. The contemplation of all that vigour churning round the park exhausted her.

On her return Carl was in the kitchen talking to Alpha.

'Come and see her have her bath.' He was as persuasive as ever. 'Beta doesn't need skin treatment.' Then, 'Glad to see you're looking good, putting on make-up and a snappy jacket like that. Your skirt could be shorter.' How personal can you get? thought Louise, but with Carl you just ignored it. The basement was the last stop on the lift, but they went down the narrow service staircase with Carl's proprietary warning: 'When you come here on your own, to wash clothes or something, don't forget to turn off the lights by the elevator. People forget, and it's a big waste.'

He led the way, his quick bustling pace not quite matching his tall, lanky body, to the far end, past a huge top-load washing-machine and an equally vast energy-guzzling drier to a couple of deep sinks with ribbed sections for scrubbing. Alpha was dumped on the ridges; her deep brown eyes, shaking body and tail curled up between her legs –

all of her living being was concentrated on this tall man who could almost hold her in his two hands. Tenderly he took her up in his right hand, stroked her with his left, and kissed her on her forehead.

'Alpha, Alphie, phie, phie, phie, come to Carl. Carl is going to rub you, to put you in a bubbly bath . . . 'and as he bumbled over her, he filled the sink, carefully testing the temperature, and added a dollop of special medicated canine skin-itch bubble bath. Or so it seemed to the amazed Louise, who had only known farm dogs who never ever got any treatment unless they were literally shedding hair with some virulent skin disease. She had never noticed that Alpha had any problems at all.

'Alpha, my lovely, Alphie, phie, phie . . . ' She was now immersed up to eyes and muzzle in white froth, pupils dilated and glued on Carl.

'She must be terrified, poor little thing,' Louise blurted out. Carl turned to look at her for the first time since the bathing ritual began, and stated, 'She loves every minute of it.' Out went the frothy water and Alphie was shivering on the ridged section at the top, held by Carl with one hand while he filled the twin sink with fresh water with the other.

'For rinsing?'' Louise queried.

Carl again looked at her in reproach.

'For a refreshing swim. Alpha, Alphie, phie, phie . . . ' Only one of the deepest pile purple towels would do to dry Alpha, who was swathed gently in foot after foot of soft thick folds. Then she emerged, damp and shivering still. Transferred to the ironing-board, she was blowdried. Carl stroked her head away from the jet of warm air, soothing her back to dry drowsiness. She was conveyed upstairs, Carl still stroking her head and flipping off the lights in between caresses. Back in her quilt-lined cane basket next to Beta under the kitchen table, Alpha began her siesta, and Carl his afternoon cigarette. He pulled the pad of lined foolscap towards him and murmured about getting the accounts up to date for 'Mamma' who would be in tonight. Deep in concentration, he began the list of numbers and pictographs that had intrigued Louise soon after her arrival, but which was still teasing her mind.

Was this the best moment to ask him, she wondered? Well, here goes, curiosity wins.

'Carl!' He looked up, then smiled. Emboldened,

'Why do you write the lists like that?'

'Because I do.' A pause. 'It's my way. Like to see?' He pushed the pad towards her and slid his stool closer so they could both scan the page together.

'That's what I bought, paper tissues, and the number. The price don't matter because it goes on the account and Mamma deals with that. She knows that I always get value, and the make she wants. Then . . . ' He travelled down the list from household supplies replenished to rooms cleaned, sheets washed, clothes laundered and ironed (a washing line with tiny sheets on it), or the birds fed (a semicircle with a stick bird below), and so on. He took a fair amount of initiative; that led to evident pride in his management skills as well as precision in carrying out the most repetitive of household tasks. Louise looked at him anxiously.

'Tell me if you don't want me to ask,' she hesitated, sensing the illogicality of what she was saying, 'but can you read?'

'Don't need to. Television and the radio tell me all what's goin' on in the world. And more!' Well, no admitting on his part, but the dealer lady's charitable efforts and the figure of 40,000,000 illiterate in the US had rooted the problem in her mind.

'Isn't it dangerous? Driving, I mean.'

'Don't drive. Don't need to. I grew up in Queens and use the subway or buses to get everywhere. I've gotten a three-room apartment, and it's stuffed full!' He giggled. 'Mamma has seen it, but she always says, "Carl, you live surrounded by shiny furniture, sparkling chandeliers, quilts over the sofa, bed and chairs, birds in cages, little dog, nothing out of place, nothing dusty, no smells. And you smoke!" You see, my home shows what a perfect housekeeper I am!' He mimicked Liz as he repeated her words, mingling admiration with amusement. He was quite an entertainer, this Carl!

Louise could be more forthright.

'I have a friend who gives time and money to a scheme to help people like you who find it difficult to read and write. Help is there, and it's free.' She remembered what Liz had told her about his spending sprees.

'Oh yeh, I've heard that story! I can read the names of streets around here, write my name. I know the alphabet. Don't get me wrong. I run the tenants' group for the apartment block where I live, prepare the accounts and deal with the owner. I help everyone, and I'm the guy that sees all goes well.

'It all started at school. My mom and dad were out working here in New York City, and we, me and my brother, didn't see much of them. My mom, she went storming down to school from time to time: "You're not teachin' my Carl. He can't read. He can't write . . . !" ' Carl gave a hilarious interpretation of his mother's forays into his school. She was evidently a colourful individual, not unlike Carl.

'They both cared, but somehow I never learnt to read and write properly.' So he wasn't a cast-off child, but maybe dyslexic? When he was young, perhaps much wasn't done about it, especially in the poorer areas.

'But doesn't it hold you back? You could get a better job . . .' Or what about the American passion for education, Louise thought. All those evening courses; all those diplomas. 'There are so many courses, in the evening. You could study to be a chef, perhaps? But not if you can't read or write. You are so knowledgeable about food,' Louise went on.

'Why should I? I got plenty of work now I'm known. Everyone likes me 'cos I do a good job. Not afraid of hard work, not me!' He smiled, then added, 'My only problem, health insurance. I haven't gotten none. OK when I'm fine, like now. But I have an *elser* and have to be careful. Sometimes people help out, like Mamma, but it could be serious.'

That's probably why he had an ulcer in the first place. Worry about health, a vicious circle.

'So I still drink a little, can eat almost anything. Anyway, I'm fine now.'

He seemed to want to talk about himself, so Louise continued,

'Don't you ever have a good time? What d'you do for relaxation in Queens?' She had no idea what that area was like. It appeared characterless when she had driven through it from the airport, but then highways create strips of forgettable buildings and littered spaces alongside. He appeared surprised at her question.

'I just live in Queens. Always have. I meet my friends in the Village.' Strange, Louise mused in her ignorance of the place and its inhabitants. She thought of Greenwich Village in terms of artists' or writers' 'lofts', of art galleries and attendant bookstores, of small cafés and restaurants with Virginia creeper covering tiny courtyards or street spaces, now empty but ready for the turn of the season when it came. How did Carl and his friends fit in there? Curiosity, once tickled, can't control itself. 'What happens there?'

Carl had started to get up; his conscience was stirring with the list in his mind of things that remained to be done. At this question he dropped back on to the stool, leaned against the wall and drummed his fingers on the table-top, giggling impishly: 'You'd really like to know? You could come this evening. I'll show you.' Louise was mischievously tempted.

'Me and the other guys meet at the Monster. It's special for us, you know. Not before 9 pm, but no later than 10.30 or 11 when the fun begins.' He paused and scrutinised her, narrowing his round brown eyes to focus beyond her almost prim demeanour. He sensed he would get the hoped-for reaction. Another giggle.

'It's great entertainment, you know, the gay bars. But we know which are the best. Sometimes we go to the shows – the drag queens, you know.' Visions of Danny la Rue and pantomime dames were conjured up, together with rows and rows of middle-aged women at Blackpool. Louise had only a second-hand television impression of it all, but was nonetheless intrigued.

'Oh, I'd like to see that.' Greenwich Village tempted her more than Blackpool ever could. Carl and his friends would make it far more entertaining. He cast another piercing look at her. Would she pass the test? Would she behave in a suitable manner? He had known haughtiness, and was cautious.

Louise explained, 'We have them, especially at seaside resorts. Women seem to like drag queens, for some reason. But it would be more interesting in the Village . . . ' Her voice trailed off as he was getting to his feet again, appearing to lose interest in the idea.

Louise remembered she had a lecture to prepare. She mounted the stairs somewhat perplexed, while Carl made off towards the dining-room muttering he would show her his apartment on Sunday, but Mrs. Daneman would have to take her.

Louise had carefully left her final days free so she could test her appetite for the last time on the Big Apple and savour the discovery of a new museum or hidden corner for her imagination to nibble at. The Sunday menu in the city was less varied, but enough remained to provide the thrill of choice, the pang of rejection. Carl's invitation had changed all that.

Liz was uncharacteristically flustered when Louise mentioned Carl's invitation. 'Didn't I tell you that he had been picked up by the police yesterday? He was late, running in the subway to catch a train, when a policeman thought he was a criminal they were out to catch. He was bolting along, and that itself looked suspicious. He has no form of identification, so they took him to the police station. It isn't required by law, so they couldn't charge him. Equally, he couldn't prove who he was. Luckily I was here when they phoned, and could tell them his name and give some idea of his address, though I don't know it exactly. I'll have to find that out before Sunday. It's scary, all the same! Here driving licences serve as identification. He doesn't drive.'

Louise was fascinated by the prospect of viewing Carl's den. It was further out from Manhattan than she had thought, a complicated journey even by subway. Liz drove over a long bridge, along streets where warehouses jostled with discount stores and petrol stations, one long service area for the city. A few stern apartment blocks punctuated this endless sequence underpinning consumer needs. Louise imagined he used a few rooms in one of them, his Aladdin's cave marooned in the nondescript.

Carl was standing outside a cut-price food store at the appointed hour. Behind the street flotsam lay leafy residential streets of yellow-brick houses with a jaunty sense of self-respect. 'That's the Italian church.' Carl indicated a large, blue-robed Madonna ascending a red-brick wall, about to speed past a jaggedly-designed blue, red and sunburst yellow stained-glass window.

The sun attempted to dispel the morning chill along his suburban street. He told them about the gangs that would be hanging around in warmer weather, the ones he had to deal with as the unacknowledged street vigilante, the single-handed 'fixer', the Robin Hood of St. Mary's Street in Queens where, 'Come summer, the older men and women will be sitting out on the street and watching their grandchildren playing around.' Louise could figure him sauntering along, tossing a remark in one direction, an observation in another, or pausing to greet others with polite concern: the lord of St. Mary's Street. Not a soul could escape his scrutiny.

He stopped Liz half-way along the row of identical houses on the right, unlocked the bright yellow front door leading into the hall and stairwell still flaunting their 1930s encrusted wallpaper, stiff with generations of yellow-brown paint. His rooms, on the first floor right above his landlady's, overlooked the small back garden. A green door opened onto a small lobby which disgorged them into a glowing green space. His living-room.

'The sofas are new. Please sit down,' he urged, adding that his favourite rag and bone man had them for sale two weeks earlier in his truck of goods ranging from fridges to chandeliers, and various furniture and fittings in between. Carl had haggled a highly advantageous exchange. He had found two wall ornaments, referred to as his 'pixies', scavenging locally – he was guarded about where and what sort of place. One was male with a ruff and harlequin's tapering hat with a pom-pom that almost hit his punch-like nose; the female pantomime half-figure bore a voluminous dress gaudily picked out in deep red, gold and blue; both were hung with a cascade of the crystal 'drops' found on chandeliers. Abandoned after their heyday, these two waifs from a procession of *commedia dell'arte* characters adorning some long forgotten music hall had at last found a new home. A large mirror over the entire wall opposite the one window reflected their drops and yellow-tongued electric candles, outflanked by the many flamed, sparkling ones of the huge chandelier, so bright that you imagined them bursting out in a flickering falsetto as Carl went over to the largest of the illuminated display cases with his prized possessions.

There they were, consigned to safe contemplation behind glass: crammed gifts of ashtrays, china bowls, pale blue and pink gold-edged Sèvres-style figurines and glittering cut-glass vases with red, yellow and white plastic flowers, and silver picture frames that protected his 'girls', his family of queens. On the low table, framed by the most exaggerated rococo swaggers of silver, were photos of his 'babies', handsome young friends. No shelf space was spare: two dark-skinned Egyptian busts in touched-up green and gold stared across the pale-green space to meet the sterner glance of a plaster Roman senator, deflected by Carl's playful daubs of green and blue to give him a disquieting squint. Lace curtains gathered in this treasure house of fancies, each dusted and cherished for its special associations – a person, a place, an event.

'Meet my girl friend. Look in here.' They were only allowed to peer in through the doorway of the inner sanctum to see a tiny Chihuahua trembling on a huge blue cushion, adrift on a king size bed. She blinked her large, liquid brown Carl-like eyes between outsize pricked ears at the two new faces next to his, then at the huge television screen in the far corner, and whimpered.

'She's so shy, Fifi, my love!'

They were steered away from the bedroom to the kitchen overlooking the back garden, to the ham sandwiches, mayonnaise and tomato, cheese and fruit displayed on the table with carefully laid plastic glasses, plates and table napkins.

Glasses of all shapes and hues crowded a cabinet above the fridge decked out with a golden rococo frame for the assorted company of magnetic figures – Michelangelo's David, Elvis Presley and Marilyn Monroe among others. As they sat there working their way through the repast, Carl extolled his efforts in the otherwise untended garden with his companion, the black squirrel. All the while he was flinging the odd endearment to his canaries and budgerigars in cages outside the kitchen window; they obliged by trilling and warbling to accompany him as he conducted the various stages of the meal.

When Liz and Louise were leaving, 'Don't you need to use the bathroom? No? Look at it anyway.'

Whether it was just to complete the tour, or to see if the two women would be shocked, they couldn't figure out exactly, but covering the walls of the cramped area outside the shower was the latest version of an 18th-century print room, transformed by wall to wall to ceiling photos. They came in all shapes and sizes and from all sources: cutouts from glossy magazines, grainy newspapers, posed photographs of every frisky scene imaginable: kisses, embraces, frolics from nudist colonies, the most outrageously-dressed drag queens imaginable – they had pride of place on the ceiling – a riot of mildly erotic fantasies to celebrate Carl's particular bent.

Liz and Louise looked considerately, for just enough time, but not too long, carefully reserving physical and verbal reactions for when they were alone.

'Here's a present.' Carl picked up a small blue, red and yellow marzipan crib from the coffee table and handed it to Louise. The colours of the Madonna hanging from the wall of St. Mary's Church which they passed on their way back to Manhattan.

Louise wondered how many others like him were stashed away happily inside the terrifying statistic of 40,000,000 illiterates. No need for the dealer lady and her crusading zeal? He had TV, Greenwich Village, the subway, a spotless apartment, affordable in Queens and filled with his treasured belongings. Carl asked for no more.

Only some rudimentary medical insurance.

Louise had to finish her work and start planning her departure; up those stairs, past the Mexican collection and the illuminated spellbinding clay figures. Her diary lay open on her desk, waiting. She started to write:

'Carl knows more than most about the "pursuit of happiness" which I know Thomas Jefferson had enshrined in the Constitution of the United States centuries ago.'

She paused, then closed the diary, placed the pen on top and gazed into the growing dusk pierced by ever more numerous specks of light. Time to get ready for the farewell dinner which her museum colleagues, so immersed in their studies, had just managed to squeeze into that evening.

for Joan and Pat

PLEASE DON'T INTRODUCE ME TO ALAN BENNETT!

We were tottering around at the time, giggling and all that, into boyfriends and pubs, when I first came across Mr. Bennett. Someone told me there was an odd sort of play on at the old Playhouse, and by a local Leeds type too. It was all over our papers. So we went, my friend Sharon and me, just out of curiosity. To have a giggle like. We'd never been to the theatre, 'cept for pantomime as a kid, as we had the cinema, and not much money anyway. We saved up, Sharon and me, as we didn't get much pay, me a hairdresser and she at our local department store. She had her bonuses, though. And me my tips. Anyway, we got the cheapest seats and saw a strange play about odd people goin' on about a dead writer and sex.

We had boyfriends at college, down on the 'building and plumbing floor' as we used to call it. They were lads who used to wait for us trainee hairdressers as we popped over to the canteen, just wait for us, stare and whistle. We'd push our chins up and strut out in our short skirts over leggings and Doc Martens. Sharon learnt to wriggle her bottom from side to side in a skirt so tight I thought would split. She were the first to find a boyfriend, the first to quit the course too. He got her into football, the Leeds United fan club to be precise, and I followed 'er, not having anythin' better to do.

Sharon wanted money, so she left to train in a big department store which I can't name. She would kill me. While she were training she came to have her hair done in her lunch break at the salon where I was doing my day release. By then I had a boyfriend too, another Leeds United supporter training to be an electrician. We looked forward to our weekly natter, having a giggle, and the experiments with Sharon's hair. She went from platinum blonde to streaky red, and at every promotion she wanted a different style and colour to celebrate. Her hair didn't grow half quick! She would turn up her pretty nose at the smell of the platinum dye an' the rinses which she said were stinking chemicals, smelling like the acid colours of the boiled sweets we'd suck at matches. The platinum dye was peppermint sharp; the red, or auburn, she preferred, smelt nasty, sort of synthetic. She liked the soft perfumes in the cosmetic department, which seemed to drift all around the store so, she explained, the clients felt relaxed.

Another difference. Our clients. She didn't tell me for ages she'd been chosen for special training, of a confidential kind, till one Friday lunch she turned up all fussed. 'What's got yer?' I was worried. After all, she were my best friend.

'It's my training. I can't say. But they want me to have what they say is a quieter hair colour, you see.'

I didn't really. I was annoyed. None of our colour experiments were meant to be provocative, so what was they going on about? We went through a number of new tints, tried one, and over the red it came out a dark sort of purple! She got into trouble and was weepy a week later. Still wouldn't tell me what was up. We lightened the purple into a regular ash blond.

It all came out a week or so later. She was always keen to earn more money, was Sharon, so she'd volunteered to train for corsetry. Not everyone's choice, you know. It's all confidential, she said, but she was told about strange goings on in the fitting-room. Then just when I were all interested like, she changed the subject. Trust Sharon!

One Friday night she came in all excited. She went on about that play by a local lad that was shocking everyone. She wanted me to go with her. She said something about people being funny in it, and then clammed up in her irritating way. That visit to the theatre changed our lives. We started to go to the old Playhouse on Friday nights when the men – her Darren and my Wayne – were out on their lads' night at t' pub.

Well, I was sort of knotted inside about it at the start. Even embarrassed when I got the idea of what was going on. There they were, these men – and women – all behaving strange like in a story about a dead writer from Prague. It was funny. You won't believe it. So funny we was holding our sides, like people around us. We began talking an' joking with them. The buzz of voices, the dresses and sparkle of the theatre, the smell and feeling of excitement when the lights dim. It sort of wraps you up into its own world.

So we learnt all about Alan Bennett from Armley in Leeds, not far from where me and Sharon grew up. We went to see his plays, and others as they come. We saved up for them. Then we begin watching out for the actors who come in and out of the theatre where the rest of us are, and find out he is one too! He actually writes himself parts!

They all look so ordinary, these actors. Even the big stars, so glamorous on TV or the papers, they just look ordinary when they come in through the theatre doors. One day we see Alan leaving, an' he comes right by us. Seems like the boy next door grown up, but still needing a hair trim and quite approachable. Except that he tries to leave in a way so that nobody notices him, like a crab crawling close to the bank of a stream. We follow him, even think of catching him up. Too late!

It was at our first night at the theatre when Sharon told me her secret. She was warned in her training it might happen, people dressing up like, but learning about it is one thing. That only happens in the theatre, we told each other, and giggled. Well, one day when she was busy thinking about Darren, a client came to be fitted with what she was taught to call 'foundation garments'. She was told always to wait outside the changing room and only go in when called. That day a curious squeaky voice called her in, and there stood the client in nothing except the corset he was trying on! I can leave the rest to your imagination. For Sharon it was for real. Her first reaction was to scream, but she'd been told to keep calm, press the buzzer, and behave in a 'serious professional way' until help came. When the department manager, stepped in, she stepped out. She wasn't really frightened, just intrigued.

On the Friday nights we can't afford the theatre, we talk about it. What would Alan have done with something like that? Seen the funny side – it makes us laugh too! Sharon got over that episode and became manager of the corsetry department – very professional she is too. I manage the salon now. We've got married, had children, but we've never forgotten Alan Bennett. Sharon an' me, we've seen lots of Alan's plays since then, in the new theatre now, the West Yorkshire Playhouse, and on the telly. The one with the Queen and the man hiding under the settee. Also we heard about the actress who played what happened to herself in real life in one of his plays. It was really weird. That Burgess and Maclean affair – spies weren't they? Alan does go in for spies and people dressing up and seeming different from what they really are!

As I washed my clients' hair – not something that really occupies your mind – I began to think I was a bit like Alan. I imagined myself working in the theatre. My hairdressing salon seemed like backstage. I was the manager getting my clients ready for their entrances, arranging them into my hairstyles. Clippin', cuttin', settin', highlightin', curlin' or straightenin', waving a wand so people could concoct a new image of themselves. That is, if their chosen style was judged successful. If not, then it was curtains for me too! If it worked, it gave them confidence in their role. Sharon thinks the same when she fits out her clients who leave feeling really great.

Then there was that book about him; we bought it as soon as it came into Smith's. He wrote a lot on funny old Miss Shepherd who camped in the drive of his London house for years. She had a caravan. He were real kind, but she gave him a ready-made character to put into his plays. She knew he was going to do that, was pleased and not pleased, if you see what I mean. Like Sharon, he seems fascinated by odd people.

What about the short plays on telly, *Talking Heads*? That's where Alan Bennett really does get almost too close to home. As I rub the shampoo into froth and look down over the wrinkled forehead of Mrs. Carey-Jones, I wonder if she might be the very one who was robbed, ever so sneakily, by her son. The smarmy creep. She's a widow too. A gentle, trusting, easily-hurt sort of type. Maybe her son's been cheating her? Did Alan know her, by chance? Of come on, don't be daft! I think as I gives the final touch to her usual hairstyle of soft, ash blonde touched-up curls, smile and pat her shoulder, and hope I'll never see that frightened look on her face. It doesn't help much either that our local vicar's wife's a regular at the salon. Whilst I discuss a new cut, I try not to let my imagination run away with me and wonder if she carries on with the communion wine like what Alan's character did. Or if she's having to put up with the boring harvest festival creations, all those brown, red and golden yellow floral arrangements round the pulpit! She's nut brown herself, so she'd fit. She looks too pushy to be on the bottle, though. Alan must have made it all up, I decide by the time Mrs. Vicar is under the dryer.

Or did he? As I brush and curl, clip and shape, my clients keep on chatting. All confidential, of course, but then, one never knows. A bit cut off here from a conversation overheard, another rebellious tail tweaked in there, and you have a dialogue all ready. Alan could shape these conversation snippets into a fine tale, I'm sure.

It makes me wonder how I'd feel. Like those Muslims who don't want to be photographed because they think it takes away their soul or something? One day, cutting up strawberries for Wayne's favourite sweet, strawberries and cream, I squeezed a bit of lemon over, and down went a pip! In and out of the strawberries I chased it, me spoon always just missing it. There it was and there I left it. Like the bit of something inside me that makes me, me. Just 'let it be, let it be,' I hummed. Still do.

There was plenty of time all week for me and Sharon to pick over such titbits and save them up for our Fridays, which then changed to Thursdays when we got married and had the kids. Our men would only baby-sit on Thursday so they had their Friday at the pub.

Me and Sharon, we stopped supporting Leeds United and instead found an evening class on modern plays, including Alan's, for ten weeks on Tuesdays, and we'd have done another if the men hadn't dug their heels in at the idea of another ten weeks of baby-sitting two nights a week! Our course teacher told us about a club, the Friends of the West Yorkshire Playhouse, as Leeds Playhouse was now called in its new building. Anyone could join, and she said we had been going long enough to qualify as Friends.

There were 'does' to meet the cast after the first night of whatever play was on. It's funny. When you meet the actors it almost seems they're still in character. I often wonder how they go about it. Do they sort of pour the character into themselves? Where do their 'pips' go when they're acting as being someone else? I wonder a lot, especially when I'm pressing my fingertips into the roots of people's hair, gently massaging the foam, releasing their tensions so they can chat if they feel like it. I even have dreamt I'm rubbing soap suds into Alan's hair, and listening to his ideas streaming out. I wonder if they come in strands like when I'm doing a hair colouring: bitty, personal scraps, their own selves, their sort of 'pips', as it were. 'Let it be, let it be.'

Sharon and I are always saying how scruffy Alan's hair is in photos. Then, would you know, we saw him at a drinks party for the cast and Friends of the Playhouse. There he was, one of the cast in his very own play. Written himself into another person, he had. I kept well back, watching him lurking by the walls. You couldn't really see his eyes behind those glasses, but I was sure they were absorbing all and sundry, especially people's funny little ways, though he pretended not to. Sort of 'yessing' and 'umming' to the people talking to him, he was, but taking it all in while they were unaware. Sort of unnerving it was.

My first reaction was to imagine giving that hair a good control clip and flip. My second, was to do his crab walk myself and hide. Sharon turned sharply to edge sideways towards the drinks table, though her glass was full. That made him glance at us with a vaguely nice but distant expression.

Safe, we walked across the hall, observing him continue his creep round the edge of the room. Some made for him, but he put his head down an' shook his hair over his forehead so it became a sort of curtain.

63

You could see and feel his eyes behind it. Sort of hungry, if you know what I mean.

We began to relax and enjoy ourselves out of range until I had a funny feeling eyes were feeding on us. Sharon had been pushing me to try out new hair colours so we was sort of noticeable. Yes, that feel of eyes crawling over us, especially her white blonde short bob, came direct from Alan Bennett himself, now only three people away. We turned and fled again to safety behind a group busily chattering. His look was so keen and sharp that it almost felt like being raped. What could he know about me? I hadn't said much, so he couldn't have overheard anything interesting. I began to worry. It must have been my imagination working overtime. Suppose he dropped into my salon for a haircut? There he might discover how I was colouring up the life of my clients, framing the features for their chosen roles. Helping them put a face on their lives. Lots of different talking heads, back stage in the salon, on stage the moment they go through the door into the world outside. A new start. From being just people, as they are, to the big buzz of the public arena. Lots of light to show up their new image.

There it was again. More than a glance. Mr. Bennett moved out from behind the group separating us. I panicked and deserted Sharon to slither behind a tall, broad Friend. Sharon found herself left face to face. A stage manager we knew introduced them. Mr. Bennett seemed so quietly kind she couldn't help telling him how she and her friend loved his plays, so they always went to the theatre if they could afford it, an' so on, an' so on. Just what I've told you about her and even more, I should think. When Sharon gets going it's like pouring water. Silly Sharon. She even told about how one morning she drove into a canal, and landed on my doorstep covered in green slime. 'I've driven my car into a canal!' That put paid to our fun shopping day in London. She flowed on an' on suchlike till the stage manager interrupted to introduce someone else. She was sure Mr. Bennett wanted the whole story. I could see from a distance that shock of hair gently nodding all the time she was blatherin' on.

If he ever writes any more *Talking Heads*, Sharon will be one of them, sure as fate. Think of someone acting her on TV without me doing her particular hair creation? Those silver tips on her favourite deep auburn flaming out around her pale face and cat-green eyes. Impossible. I'd have to be there.

Afterwards Sharon was rather perky. 'Nobody'll know it's me, except you! You and he are the only ones to suss out my secrets. I'll be dead chuffed if he finds me worth writing about,' and she struck a seductive pose. I was shocked. How could she let herself be turned into a dish for everyone to consume: writer, actor, audience? There'd be nothing left of her, not even those pips. Everything goes to them, applause – or boos. I bet he makes a packet out of the likes of her, 'cos he's known an' all that.

I've preserved my own pips in pickle. Distinct. For personal consumption only.

But – please don't introduce me to Alan Bennett!

for Stephen and James

THE MATTRESS

It is a universal truth that no Italian buys a mattress before or after Ferragosto. That's when the Virgin has her Assumption, and it's a big affair, to be well and duly celebrated. So I was looking forward to a few days of pleasantly-enforced leisure, avoiding the concentrated number of Italian Sunday drivers around 15 August. They are eagerly stalked by the *polizia stradale* strategically stationed behind cypress trees on deceptively straight stretches, the speed limit signs tastefully hidden by oleander bushes. No 'Please, Paul, let's go to . . . ' I had a legitimate excuse for three days of blissful *dolce far niente*. After all, what had I come here for, but to lie on my very special hammock under the trees, listen to the breeze, enjoy the patches of sunlight dallying from leaf to leaf before swooning on to whatever blades of parched grass remained green and upright? I swayed behind a good biography, preferably just slightly salacious, which I could pretend to read while gently dozing.

That afternoon I noted but ignored the sound of a van crunching down the drive, and strange voices, followed by the vehicle's repeated efforts to disperse the gravel when leaving.

'Paul?' Oh no. I pretended to doze behind my book, a sure sign of 'do not disturb or else . . .'

An hour later I ambled up two terraces to the familiar area around the house. Not a soul. Perhaps I had imagined the van?

Deprived of her frenetic planting activities on our visits to Italy in the spring, Helen concentrated her energies on improving the interior during our summer ones.

'We're past the primitive stage, Paul,' she had been telling me this summer. 'Our small pad here may be our hobby, but we can't expect friends to endure the mess.' That would be followed by some criticism of my untidy habits, so I cut it out of my musings.

No, something had changed. Under my favourite olive tree, centred on an outcrop above the drive, was an unfamiliar yellow object. A pile of marrows put out to dry for their seeds? Some of my mother's cast-off blankets which Helen refused to throw out to the needy, having their stains scorched off in the sun? Her irritating little phrase danced into my mind – 'waste not, want not'. Of all things it was only a yellow mattress with a faint brown pattern and duller patches provoking disconcerting unrepeatable images of strangers.

'It was left *in omaggio*.' She appeared around the bend in the drive, back from some useful errand no doubt. 'Don't look a gift horse in the mouth.'

'You couldn't have chosen a more inappropriate proverb. This is just the sort of gift horse you should look carefully in the mouth, or springs, or – and anyway, it's neither one thing nor t'other.' She understood immediately.

'A French size they say. Or one and a half.'

'What on earth can it be used for? One and a half adults? One and two-thirds children? Just like the average family which no one actually manages to have, being currently two and a fifth children!'

'Stop talking nonsense, Paul, and count your lucky stars. Here we have been given a nearly new *sprung* mattress, the best sort. The sort we normally can't afford. At least not out here. After all, this is only our hobby.' Just so. She keeps on reminding me.

'What can we put it on? It'll flop over the edge of a single bedstead, or leave a couple of feet unmattressed on either side of the usual huge Italian double one.'

It was about the time, if you remember, when the world was moving under duvets – duvets for any season even if you sweated under them; they were obligatory. At least in all the hotels we stayed in on our way to our hobby each summer. We helped the maids by stripping the cover and using it as a skimpy sheet, covering some bickering and leaving our bodily extremities for the mosquitoes to attack. Helen had been somewhat tried by fitting the vast one-metre-eighty-centimetre average Italian double bed to our four-foot-six-inch fitted sheets, and I was employed to pull the corners up round the mattress till the sheets inevitably slipped off and pinged into my face. Only when the taut sheet protested and tore was I released. Even the new one-metre-fifty-centimetre scaled down bed (*'francese'*, said our Italian friends, and winked) we had just acquired as an unaccustomed luxury, didn't take to our fitted sheets, and Helen had consequently been tetchy for some days. I was keeping a carefully trimmed-down profile.

'We'll have to find a bedstead before the shops close tomorrow for Ferragosto. Now.' I thought it better to agree, though frankly it was a waste of time and money in my view – who could ever be accommodated in an over-sized single or meagre double bed? But I wisely decided to bide my time.

She was relieved to find me less grumpy than usual about carrying the groceries and kicking my heels in the bed shop. She disappeared with the boss behind a wall of upright mattresses, and it was not long before I detected the tone of protest in her voice and quit to the street outside until summoned.

She appeared at the door.

'Paul, they have to order it specially. French size. They never keep them in stock. We'll have to wait,' she added in a pained voice. 'It will arrive just before we must leave for the start of the school term.'

'Why order it at all?' I muttered between clenched teeth, sensing an incipient drama, and hazarded, 'Why don't we think about it next spring, darling?'

She looked at me suspiciously because of the 'darling', and accused me of not realising what a generous *in omaggio* the mattress was. Nearly new. I wished they'd come and take it back. It wouldn't have been sporting to speak my mind, so I waited on.

Not one of our chorus of guests seemed to see it my way. They were standing around the new addition to our bedding on our return, making muffled reassuring murmurs of approval, sounding slightly fearful that it would have to be stored in the room they were occupying. With good reason.

The factories opened two days before we were due to leave, and the bedstead was delivered on the morning of our departure. The mattress was placed proudly on it in the largest of the guest rooms, to my intense relief – I was terrified Helen would be in an affectionate mood and suggest swapping it for our new one-metre-fifty-centimetre one which I had grown used to, but she only fussed about where to put the single bed and mattress it was to replace.

The whole matter was forgotten as far as I was concerned. I did sense she was spending the winter months plotting something, but found it to be no more than measuring fitted sheets and discussing the more boring end of domestic matters, namely of all things, bedding, with her friends. I built up a Chinese wall of newspapers, but did chance upon piles of linen with notices pinned to them: 'Paul, do NOT move or touch or otherwise molest.' Some cheek – as if I were interested!

Actually, I was. Only occasionally. Beneath all that mask of vagueness, I have a pretty practical mind, though she doesn't know it. If I do assert myself in matters domestic, or even financial, I am sharply rebuked, but that's a small price to pay for not having the hassle . . . and she does most of the income tax returns. A welcome liberation indeed, not to be sniffed at. But I did wonder about the space that surplus-to-requirements bed took up.

'They told me it was really comfortable,' Helen informed me with just a slight note of triumph the following summer. 'If it's too sweltering for our paying guests to sleep on it together –' (I should think so! A perspiring affair, and probably the male of the species would have one or more limbs over or on the tiled floor!) '– they can keep cool on separate beds, but they can be cosy on it when they feel like it.' Helen was pushing it a bit. Did we really need to go into such details? Life should be referred to in subtleties.

'What about the lurid details in those biographies you are always reading?' Helen looked at me defiantly. Could she read my thoughts, or was I speaking them out loud unknowingly? She was on that dangerous borderline of a long and ratty mood, so I murmured a sort of vague assent to I know not what and left as quickly as I could without provoking the imminent storm.

That summer Helen seemed to spend even more time with dark, romantic Romolo down in the bed store. The mattress *in omaggio* was a shrewd move. Apparently she had begun to confide in him. He commiserated with her that no fitted sheets could be found in the local market stalls or shops of the right size for the one-and-a-half-metre wide mattress he had sold her the previous summer. I was kept well away from all this, and only overheard what our guests were being told. Helen grew irritated when I hummed a silly sort of operatic tune to, 'If Romulus, then where is Remus?' or some variation of that phrase, *sotto voce* or even *forte ma non troppo*.

'*Ma signora*, you wanted the smaller bed, and Italians go for one-metre-eighty-centimetres. Obviously those are the sheets sold in the market.' And so Romolo went on to sell her mattress covers, bedstead covers, bed stiffeners – you name it, he had it. Except for the right-sized fitted sheets. No. He never sold sheets.

Those 'stiffeners' were mean little contraptions designed to put firm heart into a sagging wire net bedstead. I knew about it because I was prised out of my hammock to fit them on a particularly hot afternoon. She never chooses her moments carefully, you see, but always acts on impulse. Anyway, I obligingly snapped each end on to the bedframe, one at about shoulder height, the other beneath the buttocks of the average-length person. That average-length person, unfortunately my spitfire-tempered elder son, emerged the next morning in a black humour, with a stiffener in either hand, crashed them down opposite us on the veranda where we were enjoying a calm civilised breakfast, and rubbed his shoulders and buttocks conspicuously, with rather less decorum than should have been the case. We had guests.

'What about a bruiser bed? Any takers? I'm opting for the soft floor option, if my mother allows'. He cast a telling glance at Helen who upped to busy herself in the kitchen, nettled for once, muttering something along the lines of 'better son than guest'.

Romolo took back the stiffeners or whatever they were, and I even think Helen managed to get a refund, while no receipt was ever forthcoming. Just a few figures scribbled on a squared piece of paper with some printed logo of a mattress manufacturer. We didn't even know Romolo's surname. It was all 'Romolo' – his shop, his scraps of paper with crooked figures that passed for receipts, before a pause, and then, '*Ma signora*, if you want a real receipt, *una ricevuta fiscale*, then you'll have to pay tax, IVA. *Non conviene.*' Better not to, she agreed at the prospect of having to add over 20% to the bill which she had already accepted mentally. She may have been stubborn, but he was persuasive. And handsome, in an operatic tenor sort of way.

Fortunately the whole sheet and bed business was forced onto the back burner when the following May Helen was enlisted to take to Italy a local evening class studying Italian, to be based in a hotel not far from our restored farmhouse. It was not her style to phone me. No news was good news, she repeatedly told me. Phoning, especially from abroad, cost a lot of money. We had to save, having chosen such an expensive hobby. So I was, to say the least, somewhat concerned to hear her voice calling me in unaccustomed plaintive tones.

'Paul, oh, Paul!' My heart missed a beat. Some of the group were elderly. Had someone fallen over, ill – no, worse?

'Darling, can I . . . ?'

'They've left.'

'Who?' They couldn't. They were all on a group flight.

'Our paying guest put her hand on that mattress we were given, then poked it, and protested, "You should be ashamed to let a house with such a mattress . . ." ' A sob. Helen was referring to the people renting our restored ruin. I could cope with this.

'A refund will shut her up.' Silence, then, 'I suppose so, but what can I do?'

'Buy another bed. Get Romolo to help you. He has earned enough from us already. He'll help out.' A pause, a sniffle. 'We're losing a week's rent, and I've got to spend a lot on another mattress to replace it.' Another sob.

'Tough, darling, but life.' She agreed, blurted out that she would have to rush, that the course was going well, and she'd tell me what transpired when she got back.

It appears that it was a perfect May morning, a Saturday when one set of paying guests normally leaves and the next arrives. Helen turned up just as a middle-aged couple were packing the car.

'Please forgive me, but I think you should know, my dear, that the springs are a bit uncomfortable.' It was kindly and truly said. With the passage of time springs were emerging from the *in omaggio* mattress like a hidden debit on a balance sheet. This Helen found particularly irksome. Her friend Flavia came to drive her back to the hotel, but first they made a detour to see Romolo. 'Another mattress? Of course, *cara signora, amica mia.*' Helen was certainly his financial friend, 'but that small size, the French size,' again that infuriating snigger, 'that would have to be ordered. We don't keep them in stock. Too small for a double, too large for a single. Not enough interest . . .'

'Torniamo, velocemente!' Flavia marched the stunned and sobbing Helen back to her car and set off, breaking every speed limit there was to infringe, back to the farmhouse.

'We'll have to put your double bed in there before the new guests arrive!' Her reactions were swift, her intentions impeccable, her business sense lucid – all to no avail. The new set of guests had arrived, taken their cases into the main bedroom, where the wife had lain on the bed to rest after what she deemed a long drive in the heat. The errant coil sprang into her back, one then another, and . . . They repacked their cases and left. Furious.

'Pazienza! You'll be having other guests and they'll need a proper bed.'

I know only too well how heavy our mattress is. I had heaved it in there myself with only Romolo to help me. Helen's standards of cleanliness must have suffered as she and Flavia had to drag it out, along the veranda, round on the gravel and into the large bedroom. Then the bedstead, lighter, but hardly featherweight.

'So our bedroom is bereft of its bed?' I was concerned.

'I rang and ordered another one. Flavia said she would pay for it and get Romolo to deliver it when she could be there. I gave her our keys.' I can't say Helen sounded happy at the whole turn of events. I went down to the cellar and opened our last bottle of vintage red wine.

'Cheer up. It could have been worse.' I didn't elaborate what I meant by that.

A minute later. '*In omaggio* is in our bedroom. I'm sure Flavia will get Romolo to take it away with him.'

'I'm sure he will.' I sensed she was just about as relieved as I was.

It's not quite true to say the first thing that struck my eye when we arrived in late July, hot and sticky from a long drive in the heat of the day over the Po plain, was a large ungainly yellow hump. Under my favourite olive tree again. To dampen down the upward surge of anger, I decided not to register its presence.

'I still disagree with Romolo about the Italian proclivity for a huge double bed,' Helen declared, returning unerringly to the bed topic that evening as we were relaxing over pasta and wine and renewing our familiarity with the sunset from our veranda. I feared she might be on my track, deliberately ignoring the unwelcome presence lurking under the olive tree. Out of sight, it must be firmly out of mind, at least for our first evening.

'Romolo should have thought about it; it's his job.' Helen ploughed her topic with unnecessary vigour between mouthfuls. 'He insists Italians are so active that the heat affects them and they need space to cool off after their exertions.' There she was again, spoiling everything by being matter-of-fact. Or perhaps that was Romolo's fault. The non-existent Remus would have held him back, ha, ha!

'No time for such feeble quips,' I wisely restrained myself. As you will have gathered, I'm all for delicate, and the stress is on 'delicate', innuendo. It preserves whatever mystery might still be left in a society that untidily has everything hanging out, world-wide, on the internet.

'What's your theory then?' The wine was mellow, the simple spaghetti a dish fit for the gods.

'The whole family slept in it!' Helen declared triumphantly.

'What, three generations? Italians usually have some grandparent or other stirring the pot.'

'Haven't you seen the Great Bed of Ware?' Helen continued. 'Of course you have. It's in the Tudor room at the Victoria and Albert Museum. They're pretty certain it was used in an inn. People paid for a space in the bed, so in they piled, both ends perhaps. These Italian one-hundred-and-eighty-centimetre wide ones would have the parents at the top end, and, I suppose, the first three children between their legs. Trundle beds for extra children or grandparents were pushed underneath the big bed in daytime. They all lived in one room, remember, like the one we've divided here into living-room and our bedroom.'

That sent me off on a related tack.

'We haven't even checked whether we have a bed. You told me it was moved downstairs for the paying guests at the moment of crisis last May.'

Three cheers for Flavia. There was our squeaky-new bed, still covered in cellophane. It looked a bit tight between the blanket chest on my side and Helen's bedside table. She was throwing the clothes out of one of the cases, searching for the king-size sheets she expected would sort out the bed problem, and so sincerely did I.

'Here, Paul, take this end.' Meekly I started the whole process of putting the fitted sheet over one corner, then to the bottom. Helen did the same, but it didn't reach her corner. I dreaded the obvious conclusion – the bed was too wide. Romolo had sent the wrong size. Lips pursed, Helen whipped out of the room, returning with my measuring tape, the only one in inches and centimetres.

'It's the bigger size, not the one I had expressly ordered. Trust Romolo,' she cursed, between gritted teeth.

The general post-prandial well-being augmented by my offers to wash up, and the need to rest calmed her as she spread two flat double sheets out of the store she had accumulated from numerous aunts' houses. Mercifully there was only a crescent moon to light the nocturnal walk we always take before retiring to bed. It was too dark to spy any untoward object under the olive tree to our left as we went up the drive.

It *would* be the only morning that she woke up before me that she found the mattress. 'Paul, can you imagine it! Romolo hasn't taken the mattress away.' I nodded.

'Yes. I saw *in omaggio* yesterday. I didn't want to upset you' – but she was already on to the next thought, making plans.

'I expect he forgot. I'll make out a shopping list to buy the food before Mary and William arrive, and will pop in and deal with it at the same time.' To my immense relief I was left to clear things up at the house.

Her return from shopping was announced by an unusually sharp slamming of the car door, and rapid footbeats up the steps to the veranda. She dumped the first two bags on the table and pointed to the others, always the heaviest left for me to haul up from the boot.

'Can you imagine it! Romolo says that in Italy old mattresses are disposed of by the owners. There's no sense of client service or goodwill in this country!' she snorted.

It transpired that she had got off on the wrong footing with Romolo by marching into his emporium and demanding that he should collect and dispose of the offending mattress before her guests arrived. He took a step backwards, narrowing his eyes and, starting with the usual '*ma signora*', told her virtually to go back where she came from. Helen is nothing if not doughty – I have had a long time to realise this – so she regrouped her emotions for another sally.

'*No, signora*, when you buy a mattress in Italy, you don't have the old one it replaces disposed of for you.'

'I did in England. Bought one about two years ago from a respectable firm' – Helen hit the 'respectable' hard so it would strike a major key in Romolo's trading mentality – 'and, when they delivered the new mattress, they expected to remove the old one.'

Unimpressed, Romolo shrugged his shoulders. 'Not 'ere, chum,' or the slightly disparaging equivalent in Italian.

Helen couldn't repeat it, but she understood fully. Defeat is only remedied by renewed attack. 'Don't municipal tips exist in Italy?'

He looked perplexed, and wandered to the street door hoping for salvation in the form of new clients to rid him of this quibbling Englishwoman forever babbling on. 'What shall I do with it?' She didn't continue about it defacing the landscape, having been dumped by some unnamed person under a beautiful olive tree. He might not understand her point.

'Burn it!'

'Me? With springs? They won't burn.' She could already imagine the turgid black smoke, the stench of rubber, the irate neighbours marching down the drive. Romolo relented slightly, seeing her so perplexed, and made a helpful suggestion.

'Get Mauro to burn it.'

'Mauro who?'

'Your neighbour at the top of the drive.' Now Mauro was another story in himself, the owner of the invading chickens that had stripped our nascent kitchen garden. His prickly, easily outraged wife came to clean for us from time to time. We had put our strained relations on a better footing after some years of hostility. Better not to continue along that line, Helen concluded, nodded and beat as dignified a retreat as she could.

Our friends arrived and shared our dilemma.

'Why don't we bundle it onto your roof-rack and throw it into the tip at the dead of night?' Mary suggested. Fine, if only there existed one. Romolo said it didn't. The one we had noticed a few years earlier in the mountains had been closed.

'What about the large communal bin at the bend near the fire station?' William added helpfully, 'Where there is also a police station.' Everyone laughed. But it set us thinking. Knowing Helen to suffer from minor bouts of pyromania, I could see she was relishing the idea of a bonfire, and I was not mistaken.

'What about burning it here, on our land, at the dead of night? Nobody can control what we do on our own land.'

'Too dangerous,' I cried out speedily. 'Look at all the dry grass, and the trees might catch fire, the olives especially!'

'No! No!' our friends chorused in my support.

A midnight chore it would have to be. But where? I recalled some Italian friends telling us that one had to plop one's small-scale domestic refuse only into the one communal wheely-bin designated for your address, but we had blithely ignored their advice. We dropped our refuse in neatly tied plastic bags wherever and whenever it suited us. Or when the sight of a bin, or a whiff from the car boot reminded us of the task to be fulfilled. At the time I thought it hardly fitted the Italians' self-image of their being a highly individualistic lot. While my thoughts were loping along this track, the others were already making plans.

'We're not overlooked, but we are always getting local people walking down our drive or dropping in,' Helen noted with the glee of a natural plotter, 'so we'll have to wait till dusk before loading it on.'

'Or till dark,' Mary went even further. 'We can do it by the veranda lights.'

'The bin by the Etruscan tombs is about a hundred yards from the nearest dwelling, and isn't too far,' William added.

And so it was to be. That evening we had a meal of excited anticipation. Just after sunset I positioned our car away from the veranda, slightly frightened that Helen might have the crazy idea of throwing the mattress down on to the roof rack from the veranda. It was a heavy object. Not easy even for four relatively able-bodied people to shift.

What relief I felt to see my olive tree liberated from that yellowy, rain-or-something-stained mattress, half-lifted, half-dragged down the drive. I was not mistaken. At the foot of the veranda steps Helen paused.

'I've an idea. Wouldn't it be much easier –'

'NO!' I cut in emphatically, and wrong-footed myself as nimbly as could be. She dropped her end, causing the rest of us to follow suit.

'See,' she said gleefully to the other two, 'he hasn't learnt yet. Will he ever? Interrupting me again, as if he could read my thoughts! But he can't,' she crowed triumphantly. I persisted.

'No, it can't be lowered, or more likely dropped, from the veranda. The car could be damaged.'

Helen pouted, but the others agreed. After the third 'ready, steady, go' heave, we hoisted it half onto the rack. It would, I admit privately, have been better if we had followed Helen's idea, for it was difficult to shove it over to the far side after it had got wedged, with all the pushing and heaving, under the far rod of the rack. I didn't admit it. Instead, I went to fetch my camera. The cortège started its dignified route up the drive, past my special olive tree, down the valley, leaving the fire station and the police playing cards in the neon-lit courtyard in full sight of our allotted communal bin. We proceeded to the land of the Etruscan dead, to a T-junction, where the mountains flowed into the valley and a van usually stands in summer selling water-melons. Alone and unsuspecting stood a half-empty communal bin. I drew up as close as I could, stage-managed the way we forced the mattress under the lid, leaving enough out and flopping over the side to make a point. Away with the car, and then in a huge 'flash', Helen and friends, waving and framing the dejected mattress lolling over the edge, were caught on film before the wake.

There was champagne and delicious cakes that Helen had bought secretly that afternoon to celebrate the demise of *in omaggio*. You see, we think in harmony, well, most of the time, and a great liberation that was.

Believe you me – don't bother to look a gift horse in the mouth, just send it packing!

❧

for Faigie and Jules

☙

WARDING OFF TROUBLE

The crushed glass scattered out like shards behind Janet's stretcher surging forth determinedly over the pistachio green corridor floor. The walls were a restrained grey to cool the fraught passage of such stretcher beds as Janet's, following the white line from Reception to Glastonbury Ward 48, her temporary berth to be. She felt as if the van's headlight were still rammed into her ribs as they leapt in pain when the wheels jolted over black tape masking a cable on its way to a scan clinic, tacked on as an afterthought.

'Mornin', Jim! Back to Casualty?'

'Glastonbury. See yer, Bob!'

'How's X-ray?'

'Not so bad. Scan's overflowing.'

The cheery team of the corridor porterland floated her along and round yet another awkward turn, onto a yellow line, now curving into the next limb added to this expanding committee-designed hospital.

The last she saw of her porter was when he helped the nurses shift her painfully onto a board that slithered her, gasping, onto the bed. Pillow architecture and the drip pole became main preoccupations between offering veins for endless samples and dimly protesting at the oxygen mask, designed for an average face, that hung heavily on the bridge of her nose. One of the many nurses in a white uniform and 1950s blue elastic belt was laying her out, palm and inside elbow facing upwards to receive the life-giving liquid. Then the angels migrated, ministering wings flattened as they swooped out of sight on another mission. Or so Janet thought in slow, effortful phrases as she surveyed the three beds on the other side, as if from the wrong end of binoculars.

Her bed was near the double doors which opened onto the control area in the lobby, replete with files, computers, and figures in white overalls perusing brown folders piled on counters above cupboards. A tall elderly woman two beds down was protesting as a middle-aged, slit-skirt, powerdressed woman tried to take off her coat. Another blue-belted nurse appeared and whisked the curtains round the bed to isolate the problem, while in the next bed area an mature woman of most generous proportions poured into a voluminous salmon-pink night-dress was holding hands silently with a man half her girth. At the far end on the other side the Leeds Asian community was completely cutting off bed 23's occupant from any contact with the outer atmosphere. Three generations stood around, about ten of them, in mutely dutiful boredom.

A bespectacled figure of medium build, in a navy blue jacket over light trousers, paused at the end of Janet's bed in confabulation with a slender woman in blue, plus a few hangers-on with open white overalls.

'Where does it hurt?' A Scottish burr, reassuring in tone. How to answer when all hurt on the left side where the van had rammed her speechless in the passenger seat?

'Pain. All over. Sort of. I can't exactly locate it. It's vaguely everywhere.' He looked as if he understood.

'Tests and more X-rays tomorrow. You've broken some ribs and your collarbone. Must breathe deeply.'

He again conferred with the figure in blue, stopped at the end of the mini-ward or bay to say something to the young people hanging round him in those casual white cotton coats, and aimed for the centre of the doors, leaving them swinging out of time.

It was by now deep into the damp afternoon, not that it made any difference at all to the uniform artificial light levels inside. High tea had arrived. Someone else's order, related to the bed's previous occupant, was offered to Janet, who felt even sicker at the thought of shepherd's pie, sago pudding and the hospital version of powdered coffee. She wasn't hungry anyway.

Figures padded by, some in fawn and white patterned dresses who squeezed blood pressure out of automatic machines, topped up the plastic bags suspended from poles and took rapid temperatures with a beeping thermometer. Whenever someone approached, Janet began automatically holding out her uninjured arm.

Opposite her in berth 25 was the bay's youngest inhabitant. She had long brown hair drawn back into a pony-tail, and what looked like trendy sporting shorts striped in the same colour as her T-shirt top. Strange nightwear. Stranger still for hospital wear, especially as it contrasted with her slow bent progress towards the double doors, presumably on the way to the washroom, clutching a mysterious rainbow-coloured bag. The bed between the Indian lady and the younger one was empty.

Everyone was attached to some contraption, except for the elderly lady in 22. She had been robed in a hospital open-back nightie, but was actively mobile and anxious to talk.

'I'm Maud,' she informed Janet as she plumped herself down on the edge of the bed, setting off a wave of pain along Janet's ribs, 'and I must go upstairs to get my purse and my spectacles.'

Upstairs? thought Janet dozily. There doesn't seem to be much of an upstairs here. Maud moved to the next bed, re-arranging the yellow blanket neatly and pulling up the sheets that had been folded back in the hospital manner, watched in amazement by its voluminous inmate.

The 'cuppa tea?' trolley came round, punctuating the day at regular intervals between and at meals. It made a welcome diversion from the temperature and blood-pressure-taking, pill administration, perfunctory queries as to bowel functions, all entered in the bottle green file tucked into the end of the bed and spiced with comments about one's night habits. 'Janet slept, but was up frequently.' Or 'Janet was restless,' and so on. She had now lost the drip feed and her 'maypole' had been taken away.

'On your own to the toilet,' reassured a blue belt, Sharon it must have been this time, the freckled one.

The Indian lady had been prepared twice for surgery, then deprived of her entry into the operating shrine by a rush of emergency cases. Maud had upset her by spending part of a Friday morning tidying and then patting the blanket at the end of her bed too, leaving her nervously clutching the sheets drawn up to her chin.

'I'm just 80,' Maud told the uncomprehending lady, and then strode off abruptly towards the double doors into the lobby and the corridors with toilets and bathrooms, her strong profile determinedly heading to 'find my husband', as she informed anyone who might be listening.

Maud was not in her bed when the divine visitation took place the next morning at 8 am. That Friday morning the doors had opened, and in had come the godlike consultant, accompanied by Sister all in blue, the nice bespectacled archangel with the Scottish accent, two acolytes with open white cotton coats and a posse of student angels all straining to hear. 'X-rays showed . . . must do more . . . there may be liquid . . . otitis . . . to operate as soon as there is space . . . ' with the unexpected question tossed in here and there for one of the eager students to field. It was not an unfriendly visitation. God, that is the consultant, smiled and reassured, but his angel Gabriel, the Scottish registrar, was the one who filled in, no details spared. He had his assistants too, the house officers, who bore down on any anxious patient, and drew the curtains round to provide a confidential

81

atmosphere. So Janet had her back tapped, her queries answered, and was subtly prepared for any eventual shock to come.

All was efficiently regulated until the group moved on from Janet to the other side, past Karen the young woman with the three drainage bottles in the mysterious rainbow bag . . . ('So young to have her womb taken out . . . ' Bessie, the plump lady, had confided earlier to Janet), past the empty bed in the middle to the Indian lady. Opposite her was Maud's bed – empty! She had disappeared. Blueclad sister Jane turned pale, then crimson, wheeling round to plunge through the peering rows of attendant angels to nab the nearest nurse.

'Find Maud. Now!' But God had turned back to the Indian lady's green file, talking thyroids to his attendants, and then graced the end of worried, plump Bessie's bed. She had pains in her tummy. 'Tests . . .' to sister, by now back and taking notes again at his side, attentive, her blue eyes open in wonderment, her interpretative words to the patients reassuringly banal.

That visitation was an event to mull over in the long hours that followed, presaging a fallow weekend. 'Anyone for a paper?' came and went at about 10 in the morning before there was time to bring out the small change, and the call often got mixed up with the second round of temperature and blood pressure taking. Dull metal clattering, and along came the 'cuppa tea?' trolley, stacked with pink mugs, 'sugar and milk, love?' After all that it was handed out with fingers round the drinking edge . . .

'What's the handle for?' Janet muttered darkly to herself. And uncharitably. The tea-and-cleaning contingent were cheery to a fault.

'I aren't sure I'm a good cook . . . ' and then Bessie would pull her maypole over to Janet's bed and settle down on the comfortable chair to tell of recipes, of how her first husband had died, of her daughter, and granddaughter who always did her hair, and how she had met her second husband, 'who had seven children. He's a Catholic,' she explained. Then came pill time, then lunch, then more bedside confessions before the hour of three when the guests were allowed in.

'No more than two,' the notices proclaimed in vain to the Indian clan that came in droves, all three generations, with Neena as their mediator. She had taken time off work to translate for her mother, but found it more interesting to talk to the other patients. Young, assured and clad in a flower-patterned tunic above rust gold trousers, she told them her mother was frightened, and her operation was now to be this Friday evening. They hoped. So many false alarms. Neena viewed tall, strong-boned Maud, who had eventually been found in the next ward looking for her husband, with some apprehension. 'Mum's afraid of her. She comes and sits and talks. Mum can't understand a word, of course.' Neena's parents came from Kashmir. She had never been there, worked in the local council offices, enjoyed her job and resented having to live with her husband's family.

'Take care of Mum, please,' she begged Janet and Bessie, 'when I'm not here.'

The day ticked slowly on, light or dark outside told little on the world of bar illumination from lights on at seven in the morning to lights out at 11. The insomniacs drew the curtains and carried on their private life undisturbed, except to get a 'slept little; disturbed night' entry in their green file. After supper at 6.30, another round of checks and warnings. Mrs. Kashmir was prepared for the third time, and more generations of the family gathered, twittered, spilling over into the vacant space by bed 24. Maud, unabashed, stood surveying the Kashmiri clan and trumpeted loudly, 'Shouldn't these children be at school?' She talked on. When ignored she tended to remember her purse upstairs or her husband, and tried to go through the locked doors near her bed which led into another bay of Glastonbury Ward 48. She was always trying them, angry when they refused to open as the identical ones at the end near Janet did. From them she wandered into the lobby, fingering files and even opening the door into the room with the half-open slatted blinds and 'Sister' written on the closed door. Inside the brightly-lit room, cups of tea and coffee were brewed and toast prepared to fuel energy into the last part of the shift.

'No, Maud, not here!' So instead she spent about ten minutes straightening the crinkly elephant-grey recycled paper potties and receptacles in the specimen bathroom, one of her favourite haunts. The staff nurse Sharon had told Bessie that Maud was usually found there when she went missing on one of her jaunts.

Just after the afternoon tea shift had 'cuppateaed' the ward and then spread their once-a-week lily-of-the-valley polish over the rhubarb-coloured floor, the doors swung open and a newcomer wandered in: male, with a plastic container strapped to a belt, the tube curling round from behind his pale blue pyjama top. Its contents did not bear contemplation. Painfully thin, mobile and unabashed, he walked up and down in ghostly perusal of each bed and its inmate. Nobody took any notice. Then he wafted out again.

'I had my shower early on,' Bessie was telling Janet as she reviewed the day. In fact, between a scan and yet another X-ray, Janet had watched the to-and-froing to the toilet: Bessie waddling over after her maypole, hips dimpled and creased beneath her salmon pink nightie, or Karen, thin and bent, her large eyes etched in black like an Egyptian princess, clutching her rainbow coloured bottle carrier, making her own painful progress in the same direction. The afternoon cuppa had come, then supper with yet another 'cuppatea, luv?', and Jackie of the blue belt was ringing a bell to remind visitors it was eight. Time to go. The evening ticked on and Maud had wandered off. One of the tea ladies found her tidying up the samples bathroom yet again, and she was delivered back to her berth. A few minutes later she was over at the adjoining bed, Bessie's, to talk of her purse and her daughter; unexpectedly, she stopped, gazed at Bessie's arm, and tugged at the tube going into it from the drip,

'What's this for?' with another sharp tug at the tube close to the needle in the crook of her arm. Bessie whimpered and implored Janet, who rang her alarm button. In came Susan from the night shift.

'Now, Maud, back to bed!'

'I don't want to be next to her,' Bessie whispered as blue-belted Susan left her after checking the needle was in place, but only Janet heard.

'Just don't talk to Maud. You're too nice to people. She doesn't know what she's doing half the time.' Janet was a bit annoyed. Maud was so restless, always around fiddling by some bed, tidying up the blankets, or even running the water and playing around with it in the basin near Janet at the end of the bay, just to the right of the two swinging doors.

The Kashmiri clan had thinned out slightly, but most were sitting watchfully, their chairs turned outwards towards the door as if to protect their matriarch from any unforeseen onslaught. Neena wandered over to Karen and Janet reiterating,

'Please look after Mum. She's very frightened. I'll go with her at the start of the operation, but can't stay overnight.' They promised, though Janet was barely mobile.

The last round of pills was being prescribed when the doors swung open and a bed was wheeled in followed by two nurses. Mrs. Kashmir's turn had at last come at the tail end of the week. Her family cortège followed respectfully out of the room. The last 'cuppatea' round, the final check on temperature and blood pressure, and lights out.

'Good night, ladies!' Susan in charge of the night shift called out. Soon Maud was out of the doors, to be accompanied back a few minutes later. Janet dozed off, propped upright with pillows, only to be awakened by a figure at the end of her bed. She reached for the alarm button, but Maud moved to wash her hands by the door, and then went out. Again accompanied back, she was put to bed by a firm Susan in her no-nonsense mode.

All quiet. A slight snore from Bessie. Mrs. Kashmir returned from the operating theatre, still anaesthetised. Janet opened her eyes, wondering if she had to make her nightly jaunt to the toilet when she saw Maud's gaunt silhouette pause at the foot of Karen's bed and – a long moan opened into a yell punctuated by sobs. Janet reached for her alarm button. A nurse came in and made for Maud. It seemed she had pulled out all three tubes in an urge to tidy things up, leaving Karen howling. Susan followed the nurse, pulled the curtains round, and consolingly dealt with Karen's drainage tubes and attendant griefs. Maud stood stranded in centre bay, undecided what to do next. Janet was terrified. Bessie lay still, but was surely awake. The nurse who had come in first was watching Maud. She had long curly hair, was of medium build and firm demeanour. After a long pause, she touched Maud on the shoulder.

'Maud, you must stay in bed.'

'Don't you dare touch me. I'll call the police!' A pause. 'You can't do this to me!' The tall 80-year-old pushed the nurse, then grabbed her hair crying, 'Out of my house!'

Janet pressed her alarm yet again. Susan emerged from the gap in Karen's curtains to see what was happening, and grappled with Maud, freeing her hands from the nurse's hair. Two more shadowy figures rushed in.

'Don't touch the nurse, Maud.'

'She touched me first. Anyway, I didn't touch her. This is my house.' Two figures accompanied her, still muttering, to her bed, but she was clearly too agitated to stay there. Karen was sobbing and Bessie whispering that she couldn't remain next to Maud. It wouldn't be safe. 'Time to move,' thought Janet, and painfully swung her legs over the side of the bed, wriggled her toes into the non-slip hospital slippers and went out into the lobby. Susan was behind the range of computers, glued to the phone. Janet pinned her gaze on Susan till she replaced the receiver and looked up questioningly.

'We can't sleep with Maud in the same room.'

'I've been trying to find another bed for her, but the hospital is full.' Pass on the problem, thought Janet. But she felt she had to speak for everyone, and especially Mrs. Kashmir, who was attached to what seemed to be numerous post-operational drips, or to Maud, bits and hanging bobs that needed tidying up.

'We can't have her in there with us.'

'I know. Please go back to your bed. We will cope.'

'How?'

'I aren't sure. Please go back. One of the nurses is with Maud. It's quite safe. Please . . . '

Janet slowly hobbled back to berth. Her lights were out but Karen was still gently moaning behind the curtains. Now in her curtained cubicle, Maud was complaining loudly that she had never hit anyone and, anyway, what were people doing in her home? More whisperings, then in came Susan briskly propelled by orders from on high. A few minutes later Maud, lying like Cleopatra on her barge, was pushed out of the bay by two night porters, destination unknown. An anxious silence lay over the remaining four occupied beds, as Mrs. Kashmir was stirring.

'I'm frightened,' whispered Bessie. 'She's somewhere outside, wandering around, fiddling. I want to go to the toilet, but daren't.'

'I'll go and see what's happening,' Janet offered, as she knew they hadn't been able to pass the Maud problem on to another ward.

In the lobby Maud's bed was moored to one side; blue-belted Susan behind the computers and close to the phone was keeping watch.

'Don't worry, please, Janet. Everything's under control. Please go back to bed.' She did, after visiting the toilet.

'All seems safe,' she confided to Bessie on her return. 'Maud is awake, but in bed and watched.' So Bessie's silhouette billowed across the bay propelling her maypole mast before her to the toilet.

The night passed, anxiously. Neena was in early to see her mother, and was quickly told of Maud's assault on the nurse, not to mention her 'tidying up' of Karen's tubes.

'What about Mum's?'

'Exactly,' Janet and Bessie nodded. 'Besides, they rolled Maud's bed back to her bay early this morning. Without her, fortunately.' It was assumed that Janet would be their spokesperson.

'I'm not staying here if they have Maud back,' Karen declared understandably. She had hardly stirred from her bed since the incident and hadn't even had her cubicle curtains fully drawn back. It was Saturday now. No heavenly visits, unless there was a medical emergency. Janet went out to see Sister Sarah on the weekend morning shift. She looked up so cheerfully that Janet felt she was the unwelcome bearer of awkward news.

'I have been asked to say for all of us in the bay that we can't have Maud back, after what has happened. Mrs. Kashmir has returned from her operation with a drip-feed affair, and others have tubage of one sort or another. Everyone's worried because her bed has returned.'

'Of course we put the health and safety of you all first,' Sister Sarah smiled automatically, 'but look at Maud now. What's wrong with her?' True enough, Maud was meekly sitting at a table set for her in the lobby, staring into space over newspapers and magazines that had been placed in front of her. Apparently she was in for tests, just when her only daughter had decided to go away for a week to Lanzarote. She didn't want anything done to her mother until she returned. So Maud was marooned in hospital, sat down in front of papers she couldn't read because she had brought the wrong glasses with her. And she was 80 yesterday. Or about to be 80 tomorrow, she wasn't quite sure.

Janet reported back, and decided to combine more walking, as she had been advised to do, with a running account to the others of Maud's behaviour in the lobby. Mrs. Kashmir had received a fleeting visit from her husband that morning, when he chanted over her and raised his arms towards heaven. He then left rapidly. Neena too. Her mother had sunk back into the sheets, her small brown head framed by a long plait that snaked under her chin and down the other side. Janet, again exercising, decided she must try to communicate.

'Maud,' and she pointed at her empty bed, 'is being watched over outside. We won't let her come back after what has happened,' and she waved her uninjured arm in what was meant to be a negative gesture. A slowly beautiful smile of relief intermingled with gratitude started in Mrs. Kashmir's eyes and spread over her face. She raised her hands in a praying gesture, and looked upwards. Janet followed her. Communication complete – as far as it could go.

The remains of the lily-of- the-valley polish were wearing off beneath the weekend lethargy, and the scent was turning into acrid anxiety. Even the normal converse on matters medical was dampened, silences punctuated by the metallic patter of the 'cuppatea' trolley with the much-fingered pink mugs, or the resonant clanging of a tank-like vehicle. It lurched forwards with the hospital meals of stews, shepherd's pie, casseroles and sago or sponge pudding or a treat of melting vanilla ice-cream if you were a lucky diabetic, and all heralded on the order form by their letters: F for fibre, V for vegetarian, D for diabetic. These sounds all differed from the pert click of the pill-dispensing trolley, or the giddily revolving caster wheels conveying the blood-pressure machines on their stands. A mild diversion came that Saturday when a heavenly command banished forever the squeaking underarm thermometers in favour of the undertongue sheath method, creating the need for a slot to keep one's very own thermometer cover. This also pinged when ready, marginally more quickly than the underarm variety.

Mrs. Kashmir had her usual three-generational cohort around her that afternoon. They made up in numbers for what seemed to be lacking in conversation, as, the younger the members, the less they could communicate with granny in her Kashmir variant of Urdu. Now reigned a half-lit inertness with a strange and ominous sense of expectation.

The supper 'tank' rumbled in, almost colliding with the perky 'cuppatea' trolley. Change of shift, and not the same one as the previous evening. Bessie had been enthusiastically telling Janet, who was averse to cooking of any kind, the best of her recipes and what she gave her second husband at Christmas in contrast with the first, while Karen, encouraged by all, had been able to go to the toilet and even ask for help with a shower. Janet thought her a quiet, even furtive type, with a strange range of sporting nightwear, and a 'partner' who always drew the curtains round when he came to see her, exciting Janet's imagination but passing unnoticed by Bessie. Mrs. Kashmir couldn't notice anything as her view was entirely blocked by the silent members of her clan exuding as ever listless resignation.

Bessie clattered her maypole over to Janet's bedside, sighed, crammed herself into the allocated guest chair and blinked.

'I had a good shower this morning and washed my hair. It's all frizzy now, but my granddaughter did a good perm.' She paused, as if worried to add anything. 'My pains are getting stronger and they never seem to manage to get my tests done.' Another pause, and she looked long and pleadingly at Janet. 'What's going to happen about Maud? Her bed's here, and she has wandered in twice.' At the mere mention of Maud's name the air bristled.

Four pairs of hostile eyes had followed Maud in her red dressing-gown as she strode through the swinging doors and made straight for the empty bed whose inmate, Anne, was spending the weekend at home. She then veered towards Karen, who clutched her rainbow bag and the alarm button, ready to act, then wavered.

'Maud, that's not your bed,' Janet hurled at her from her berth, while pressing the alarm button. She sensed that the nurse who came was slightly irritated to be summoned just to accompany Maud out. It didn't somehow fall into the category of her nursing duties. Janet needed to find out what would happen to Maud that night, now that her bed was back in its cubicle, even if without, as yet, its occupant. The new night nurse, Jackie, commander of the evening shift, was robust and determined, a veteran of twenty years' night duty.

'Yes, we know what happened. There are no beds anywhere else. We'll wheel her bed out later on and she'll sleep outside. There's no room to keep it in the lobby during the day.'

Janet reported back, to the general relief of the four in the occupied berths. A quiet night would follow, as quiet as any when each was locked into the prison of her own medical anguish.

Janet dozed off late that evening. Though the Scottish archangel declared that it was not their medical policy to dole out sleeping pills, she was convinced that some sort of tranquilliser was blended in with the evening dose of pills, though each medicine had, as was now medical practice, been over-fully explained to each patient. 'Lucky we are still patients, even if impatient, and not yet clients or customers,' mused Janet, suspended between waves of oblivion and a deep pain in the lower part of her back. Then she slipped into a dream: she was stepping lightly in a hilly landscape with lakes and waterfalls, and streams that gurgled and fell over clear rocks. She heard running water.

Then silence, just some heavy breathing from Mrs. Kashmir, and an occasional snort from Karen. Was that Bessie going towards the door carrying something strange in one hand while pushing the maypole with her drip-feed in the other? She waddled slowly towards the doors, her left hand propelling the maypole, the other holding a strange protruding object, of no easily recognisable shape. Instead of aiming for the middle of the doors, she veered to the right, splashed something from her right hand into the basin the doctors used, turned, and paddled slowly back to berth.

By now Janet was wide awake. Perched indignantly on the horns of a dilemma, she painfully swung her legs over the side, toed around for the unslippable slippers, and made her way slowly to the doors. Outside someone was talking to Maud who evidently wouldn't lie down. Ample, reassuring Jackie was installed by the computers and the rest were making toast behind the window slats and the closed door with 'Sister' on it. They would be discussing the 'Maud case', probably sensing a growing anti-Maud conspiracy in the bay, launched by Janet in berth 20. She had seen the way each shift briefed the next, and between the pills and need for scans, X-rays or barium meals, would be the interjection, 'Watch bed 20. Always criticising . . .' She would be classed as 'to be watched. A possible ringleader'. Janet feared she might now be seen as 'telling tales' or something, though –

'I don't want to be a nuisance, but as this is a place that exists to promote health . . . ' her voice faltered. Jackie looked up, not unkindly. 'I, I saw Bessie empty a chamber pot into the basin in our bay. I'm worried.' Jackie looked aghast. 'I'll see to it,' and disappeared into the sister sanctum. Janet continued to the toilet, checked on the way back that Maud was still safely in her bed moored inconveniently in front of the control desk, and then through the swinging doors to bed. A few minutes later, as she was dozing off, a figure appeared by her bedside. She was about to scream, fearing it would be Maud, when Jackie shushed her silent.

'I just want to tell you we have put bleach down the basin twice and run water through it. Oh, and we've taken the pot away from under Bessie's bed.'

Early that morning Bessie was freed from her maypole. She was radiant, even though the pains continued to rumble around in her belly.

Sunday saw predictably the biggest inrush of guests. Janet could never understand why she didn't notice Maud's berth being rolled back into its corner, and Maud herself installed. It may have been because mid-afternoon she had been horribly fascinated by the re-apparition of the thin man in pale blue pyjamas and bottle of bodily fluids hanging prominently at his waist doing his rounds in the ward, still ignored by everyone. Or because, still later, Anne retook possession of berth 24 opposite Bessie, and was updated on the Friday night drama by Janet and Neena together. Anne was an amusing, leathery 50-plus, with a grating laugh, swollen stomach and flavour of tobacco about her. Bessie was registering a high level of distress, fearful that Maud, who didn't have many visitors, would soon be hovering by her berth, the next one along. She understandably felt she was in the front line.

'I haven't got my drip any more,' Bessie tried to reassure herself, 'but I'm afraid she'll do something odd. Especially at night.'

Janet felt herself once more the unofficial leader of the bay, the one who had to confront the staff yet again with the Maud question, seeing she had been surreptitiously slipped back into her berth without their agreement. To Janet while at Anne's bedside, Neena had stressed how worried she was for her mother, unable to explain anything much in English, still with a tube attached and in a delicate post-operative state. She, Neena, had a lot on her mind, what with having to live in a hostile family, her husband's, which didn't want her to work. She had

had to give up her personal car and let it go into the family 'pool'. She didn't want to give up her independence with a good job and generous maternity leave. Karen, who had been told before the Maud incident she could leave once her drainage tubes were taken out, feared she wouldn't now be home for her son's birthday. All had been set back by Maud's obsessive need to tidy those irritating tubes. They couldn't run the risk again. Janet would have to find out what was happening to her. Bessie had seen a younger woman briefly at Maud's bedside, then the fashionably-dressed one who had a hospital identification card on her, but they had gone and Maud had stayed quietly in her berth, hardly moving, even sleeping a little.

Out Janet went in search of the nurse in charge. Weekends were hopeless, with no one she knew. She waited outside 'Sister's sanctuary' until a senior-looking staff nurse emerged.

'Do you know about Maud, bed 22?'

'Oh, yes. Anything the matter?'

'We were promised that the four of us, or five now bed 24 has returned' (that was how they knew the patients primarily, bed number) 'that our interests came first, and that Maud wouldn't return.' Janet could sense that she was being judged unreasonable, or as one spearheading a revolt which was quite unjustified. 'She did assault a nurse. And pulled the tubes . . . '

'I know that,' the staff nurse interrupted, 'but she has had visitors, and they can't see a patient in the lobby.' She squeezed her cheeks into a quick smile and turned to get on with the next job in hand. Janet felt snubbed. She had also let the side down, as Bessie's eyes emphasised on her return to say that Maud was back to stay. It would have helped if she had been told there and then what Jackie, once the night shift was back, later explained. Maud, it seemed, had been creating tensions, wandering into other bays, picking up files, back again 'tidying' the bathrooms and the grey recycled chamber pots. Her granddaughter had protested at seeing her in the lobby. The night staff were well primed to any possible unrest, and, anyway, Maud had calmed down somewhat. She had been found to be diabetic three weeks earlier, and the wrong dose of appropriate medicine had been prescribed. Now they were sure they had found the right balance.

So Maud was back. Jackie of ample girth settled bed 21, and Bessie was reassured that she would get her scan come Monday, Karen that her tubes would be out then, and Mrs. Kashmir that she would be back home within the week if only she would try to walk a little more.

She preferred to sink into her bed, two frightened eyes framed by the dark, grey-streaked plait, eloquently suffering in silence. Lights off. All quiet. Maud back in berth.

Janet sank into sleep, not knowing whether she had dreamt or seen a tall gaunt silhouette make for the swinging doors. She did, however, sense she had to make one of her twice-nightly visits to the toilet, and so made off for the swinging doors and her favoured bathroom along the corridor which led to another bay in Glastonbury Ward 48. She knew the way in her sleep, almost. Back through the dusty light, past Jackie perched at command control, a quick glance to imagine the exchanges behind the window slats and the half-open door of 'Sister's sanctuary': 'We've got Maud back. Nasty of them to gang up against her. She's not a bad old bat, really . . . ' Janet blinked such ideas out of her mind which was burdened enough with illnesses, hers and those of all the other berths minus, curiously enough, Maud's. Through the swinging doors and back to her berth, nearest to the doors beyond the basin on the left. As she slowly approached she was surprised to see the yellow blanket was neatly folded in a rectangle down the middle of the bed. Strange, because anyone in pain and with limited movement and a tendency to feel the cold like her would spread the blanket carefully over the whole bed to cover every part of the body. Closer, her hand out, she stopped in horror. The bed was occupied, the incumbent gently snoring.

Out through the swing doors to find Jackie. The command desk was deserted, as were the lobby and the corridors. 'Sister's sanctuary'? She knocked firmly on the closed door. Silence, then it opened and one of the weekend agency faces peered round.

'Maud's sleeping in MY bed!' Janet's words were repeated to hilarious effect to the crew inside.

'I want my bed, clean sheets, to sleep in . . . ' Janet's voice was unnaturally shrill. Out emerged competent Jackie giving orders, and whispering aside to Janet, 'You're probably lucky. I once had a male patient who would seek out empty beds, pee in them, and then return happily to his own dry one.' Thus 20 years of night nursing experience!

Janet stood and ached while Maud was woken and led, mildly protesting as she had been sleeping so soundly in Janet's, to her own bed. Bed 20 was stripped and relined with lavender-scented sheets, or so Janet imagined in search of imaginative relief.

Next morning, just after the 8 am celestial Monday visitation of God the consultant and his heavenly hosts consisting of the Scottish archangel, two seraphim as house officers and attendant angelic students dispensing energetic orders of hope or fear for the week entering, Bessie sat down by Janet and asked what all that laughing had been about during the night. It had woken her up. In the cold morning light, she and Janet discussed the neatly folded blanket. One of the nurses was guilty of tucking Maud into the wrong bed. She should have known better!

'Why can't they inform the nurses properly who's in what bed when they start the shift? I accept they may have new ones from an agency, but they have to be told basic details about each patient, and we're all ultimately linked to our bed number. I'm Janet number 20; you Bessie number 21, and so on. Maud would have been number 22.'

Number 22 was by then out on her barium meal scan; Janet was soon wheeled off to another X-ray, and Bessie to her scan. Expectation laced with apprehension invaded the oxygen of the ward that morning. It was a potent mixture, enhanced by the renewed insistent syncopation of the 'cuppatea' trolley, the 'tank' clattering around with meals which started the week better than they ended it, and the pinging of the more discreet pill trolley. The sheath thermometer that had usurped the role of the underarm one, created mini anxieties when the cleaning ladies forgot to replace the suction sheath-holder on the cupboard side, next to the out-of-date names of each patient's nurses and the paper disposal bin for swabs and discarded tissues. New urgencies, and the rumour that everyone was to vacate this bay to let it return to male dominion, as it had been a week or so earlier.

Janet couldn't get over her irritation at a nurse mistaking the bed. She found one of the nurses who had seemed of a slightly more available turn of mind, and waited patiently for her to get off the phone.

'Why was Maud put into the wrong bed?' she asked, after explaining the incident in case she had not been told at the shift turnover briefing. But she had.

'No they didn't. Maud mistook the bed.'

'Impossible,' Janet insisted, emboldened as she wasn't speaking to anyone whose shift could have been guilty of such an elementary error. 'The blanket was so neatly folded, in a rectangle, and placed over her from shoulder to toes, just the top of her body. Quite strange, really.'

'Maud folded it over herself in that way.' There was no more to be said. The nurse had a lot on her mind, propelling the week forward. It was Monday, after all.

The others who hadn't had their bed invaded were beginning to feel kindly towards Maud who, since Sunday morning, had been quietly staying by her bed, except when on a voyage to the toilet. Perhaps it was because they felt guilty of having unjustly disliked her. The prospect of going home does damp down emotional reactions it seems.

The bay was returning to its former male identity by divine diktat. Karen, Mrs. Kashmir and Maud were going home. Bessie, Anne and Janet were off to a neighbouring bay. All their possessions had to be on the bed by suppertime. Maud was gathering her belongings under the supervision of the smartly-dressed lady from the X-ray department, who turned out to be her daughter's friend.

'Did Maud fold that blanket so neatly and strangely over herself?' Janet asked her.

'Of course not. How could she? She was under it, after all. What an idea!' Everyone laughed. That afternoon Maud's daughter had returned from Lanzerote and so could deal with her mother, who had had the tests that very morning.

'Just so!' thought Janet, as she slowly ordered her few possessions on the bed and readied herself for a new berth. On to the next episode. She was already beginning to miss Maud.

The Campo, Siena

for Anne and Sophie

SPACE

The sun is behind you, reader, the Palazzo Pubblico beneath you, as angel-like you zoom down to me, that space on the left of the Fontana Gaia in Siena. The shadow of the Town Hall tower has passed over me bearing the growing gaggle of spectators with it. Problems started when the shadow was just to the right of the fountain sometime after midday. My space by the temporary barrier in the sixth section of the shell-shaped square is already cluttered with back-packs and bundles. Their owners think they can colonise my space and then stroll off to amuse themselves elsewhere. The herring-bone pattern of the burnt-Siena bricks is still visible. A bit of my space between the backpacks by the barrier is still free, perhaps only a carelessly ignored half-metre or yard, what you will, but an older woman spies it immediately. 'Here's a space. It hasn't been taken and it's near the start,' she mutters to the dark-haired one behind her, followed by a young girl in shorts toiling beneath a heavy knapsack.

'Let's line up behind one another; we'll only need a narrow bit of space. We're lucky!'

'People come so early!' exclaims the dark-haired one, 'there's still five hours to go before the Palio starts.'

'And waiting in the sun too,' adds the teenager, commenting that they have by now missed the brief respite of the shade from the Torre del Mangia.

The older woman opens up a small canvas stool and settles down with resignation founded on experience, leans against the wooden barrier and surveys the famous Palazzo Pubblico, already at home in my space.

'Pray for a cloud or two. Or just for one little cloud!' She calmly dons a wide-brimmed hat, opens a book and a lined pad to make notes, and settles down into me.

I am soon disturbed by a girl straddling some bags and newspapers on my right. She yells in Spanish that the space is taken. The usual kerfuffle I've heard so often before, with the obvious rejoinder that no-one is here, so the space is free. Just so.

'There was somebody in that space before; he's only gone away for a moment,' the voice continues in Spanish, which I sense the older woman understands; her leg muscles stiffen as she stabs at the pad with greater determination. The litany of protests is taken up to the left by an Italian voice with a Milanese accent. I am not up for grabs, so to speak; someone has already laid claim to me.

'There was nothing and nobody here,' replies the older woman in Italian, and goes on writing. Her dark-haired companion sits down in front of her and opens a book, while the girl in shorts squats on my herring-bone bricks and scrabbles around in her knapsack. All seem to be nicely settled. So far, so good.

'He's only away for a short spell,' the Spanish voice again.

'He'll be back in a minute,' an Italian voice, adding, 'Place not free,' in English. The three seated figures are resolutely silent. Six youthful figures in a rough semi-circle around them are projecting a concentrated visual condemnation of the way that bit of my space has been occupied. To no avail.

Calm reigns in my space for a good forty minutes, then – 'Get out of MY SPACE,' in Spanish, uttered by a chunky male, thirty plus with glasses and designer stubble. His eyes pierce me, splintering the hot air as he orchestrates the stabbing hostile Spanish, Italian, English phrases from his supporting cast.

No reaction from the three seated. Infuriation always stirs me up. The Spanish voice returns to the attack, this time in English.

'We shall call the police!'

'Faccia pure!'

The Spanish man turns away frustrated. I sense the older woman is gradually losing her cool as the aggression increases. Her writing is becoming jittery, and she's furious that anyone thinks he can own me, a public space. She whispers to her dark-haired friend that on three previous Palios she has left her bags by the barrier, only to find someone had removed them and taken the place. She continues louder in Italian,

'You can't keep the space here and just go away and do as you will. This is public space, free for all!' So be it. Her friend agrees. It is hard, the older woman admits, to stay in one place for hours on end. When she once brought a young child here to see the race, he had to relieve himself into an empty Coca-Cola can because by then the whole square was seething with people and they could hardly move an inch!

Now it is totally different, the older one continues. At least half a yard on the barrier was free when we three arrived, and we can stand behind one another like a spoke down into the square, leaving plenty of elbow room at the barrier for the groups on either side. The taller folk can stand behind the smaller ones. It's common sense. They'll come round eventually.

I hope cooler judgements will prevail. They don't call the police, of course, but a Milanese actually grabs the older woman's leaf-patterned plastic bag and runs to the centre of the piazza, twirling it triumphantly round his head. No reaction on her part. I sense the belt with her money and documents safely round her waist. Her work is in that bag. No use to anyone. This act of bravura falls into bathos, and the bag is dumped. The young girl puts her sketch pad down onto the bricks below me and goes to retrieve it. They say little, these three, all busy in their own ways. The older one goes on making notes, the dark-haired one reads, and the girl starts a water colour of the Town Hall. They sit facing down into the square, their backs towards the periphery barrier, occupying their small spoke in the larger plan of my square's activities.

It's well past two and the heat is almost unbearable. Not far from the Fontana Gaia two stalls are doing a brisk trade in mineral water and every commercial brand of soft drink. The crunch of plastic or tin underfoot is now commonplace. Inevitably the usual water horseplay starts; the more sophisticated have brought their water pistols, others make do as ever with open plastic bottles. Jostling by the fountain for refills, or on the sand-covered track, gangs contrive mock battles, soon bespattering manure-hued sand stains over their designer shirts, shorts and trainers.

Two-thirty groans on to three, and attacks are renewed on the hapless three intruders, or rightful occupiers of public space – in other words, of me. Imagine: the entire contents of water pistols and plastic bottles pouring onto the three women, mostly the older one, being the perceived ringleader. The notes, book, unfinished water-colour are all hurriedly put away. Other refilled water pistols and plastic bottles are being diverted onto the routing revellers on the track; then their aim is swung back onto the so-called 'chief intruder' in my space, drenching her from nape to buttocks as she sits, back to the barrier, unmoved. Beneath her camp stool a puddle is gathering, suggesting a lack of other restraint. Unaware, she smiles around and announces, mainly into space, that she likes being showered. So cool, so pleasant. The attack dwindles into a dribble. The puddle beneath her stool has dried up by three-thirty.

A noisy, gesticulating crowd is gathering down by the chapel tacked on to the Town Hall many centuries ago. Squeals of delight as the water hoses are turned on to dampen down the sand in expectation of the parade to come. The pied piper lorry moves slowly round the track spewing water out over an increasing crowd of reckless devotees. Shrieks as a cannon fires. Four o'clock: the Head of each *contrada* is putting the final touches to his Renaissance garb, mounting his draught horse, and preparing to lead the procession of standard bearers, weapon bearers and flag-throwers into my piazza. The nervous racehorses are now being blessed in each district's church, the embodiment of streets of hope. Quivering, nostrils dilated, and an hour yet to go.

Four-thirty – still hardly a cloud in the sky. Another hour before the sun sinks towards the cathedral and puts me into shade relief. No relief from clutter. Unimaginable. Worse this year than ever. Indescribable how the bags, back-packs and newspapers join discarded bottles and cans of all shapes and sizes. The air is stale with tired bodies pushed together, huddling to keep out sneaking infiltrators. A pick-pocket's paradise, except the people worth picking are only now beginning to appear on the stands in front of the shops on the other side of the damp sand track. Nothing for them to survey except the horseplay of sweaty bodies wearied by the pervasive sense of stagnation. Too long to wait: too little to do. Peaked caps mark the decline of spirits; peaks swivel round to provide scraps of shade for reddening necks, leaving absurd semicircular lunettes above eyes, elasticised bands tightening their sweaty hold on throbbing foreheads. Heat, smell, dust into dirt; too many bodies crammed into my space, and now more people gathering on the stands peering down, vacantly curious. Eyes all over me; another more powerful electronic one scans into the tension between the Spaniard and the still seated older woman, who finds muscled calves pushing and easing her over while the Milanese contingent, unaware, hear her apologising in Italian when she is forced to lean into them.

The young girl is embarrassed by all this. The dark-haired one whispers advice to her older friend:

'You'll have to watch out when you turn round to face the racetrack; he could easily edge in.'

'I know. I'll have to wait until he gets tired of trying to heave me over.'

As he pushes his legs against her, the older women attempts to press them back into their place. The hairs on the Spanish calves bristle out in angry determination as they thrust hard again, almost toppling her off the stool. Outmatched, she resorts to stabbing them with her pen. Air buzzes with heated, pent-up anger. The older woman always replies in Italian, so no one knows her nationality. In desperation the Spaniard roars, 'British colonialism all over again!' No response. Does she understand? They think they hear her whispering to her friend in English. Air impregnated with furious uncertainty. Then, after a long pause, she comments softly, in Italian again, 'Who are Spaniards to use such out-of-date anti-colonial arguments?' He is probably too angry to listen.

The intense scrutiny of the TV camera swoops down on me again. The commentators, one male, one female, are gabbling into microphones. She concentrates on a balcony where a vivacious red-haired woman is talking animatedly to champagne-sipping companions. Hand on her shoulder, the elderly host is pointing out parts of the square. Fashion-conscious figures saunter nonchalantly onto the stands, and the female commentator obligingly concentrates on their self-display. The male one surveys the sweaty masses seething all over the terracotta bricks so that not an inch remains unsullied by this crowd, a writhing, multi-coloured, freckled monster, about to erupt from tedium.

The Spaniard shifts his calves over yet again to meet the poised pen when – her stool collapses under the strain of events! The older woman's shoulders are heaving up and down into the little of my space that remains, and I wonder if she is sobbing. But I soon feel her friend's shoulders moving in the same way, both trying to control their laughter.

'Shall I pull you up?' the dark-haired one whispers.

'No. Wait for a moment when I can swivel round.'

All this is studiously ignored by the young girl who has pulled her cap over her eyes and is trying to pretend she doesn't know them as she doodles on a scrap of paper tucked between the pages of her book. Anticipation of the race is dragging on too long.

A scuffle breaks out further down on his left and the Spaniard turns to look at it; the older woman neatly rises to her feet, swivelling to lean over the barrier.

'No, no, no!' yells the frustrated man, jabbing his elbow at her.

'Watch out!' cries the dark-haired woman, 'You'll crack her jaw!'

'Out! Out! Out!' he is chanting, shoving the older woman towards the section of the barrier held by the Milanese group who are looking on warily. All for about half a metre of my standing space by the barrier!

The eye of the TV camera deserts the vivacious redhead to swoop down on the dark Spanish head bobbing up and down in a furious crescendo of stale insults accumulated during the five hours' contest for my space. His final tirade orders the older woman to retreat to the centre of the square where she belongs. She remains unmoved, just looking up to contemplate the male and female commentators framed in the window opposite. A pause. Another cannon blast announces five is striking; the spectacle is about to start. The multi-coloured freckled monster ripples smoothly outwards towards the barrier; excited expectation cooling voices and soothing nerves, transforms into a buzz of fresh anticipation and undiluted enjoyment.

The Spaniard pauses in his tirade.

'Have you finished" asks the older woman in Italian. He looks puzzled. 'Can we have a calm word?' She continues, 'Which language do you prefer – French, Spanish, Italian or English?'

'I can speak them all. I am a true European.'

'Join the club,' declares the older woman, pulling her bag and broken stool from under her legs to make more space for the Milanese group on her right. 'All I need is just this short bit of the barrier – please let me finish – which was empty, so that this young girl can stand in front of my friend. You order me to retreat to the middle of the square. Fine. I'll go there. I've seen the Palio before. All I want now is to give this young girl a good view, which I've never managed to have myself.'

'If you had told me that when you came, then she could have had the place.'

'You were so angry,' replies the older woman, 'and, in any case, was it really yours to give?'

'I did stay here all night to keep it.'

'How was I to know? We didn't touch anything – there was nothing there to remove. This narrow strip was empty. But, please, don't let's argue. Here she is, and my friend behind her. They leave plenty of room for you and your friends to see everything.'

The Milanese on the other side are relieved as the atmosphere freshens. The first band is drumming and blaring out to our left. The camera swivels round stabbing the air in its direction while the stands are slowly filling up and the vivacious Duchess of York leans over the edge of the balcony to wave. The spectacle is on.

'What's your name?' asks the older woman. 'Carlos? This is Julie.'

The young girl is much prettier now she has taken the peaked hat off and loosened her ash blond hair to frame her flushed cheeks. The sun is descending behind the stone tower to their left, casting its last golden rays over the cathedral district. The evening resuscitates new hope, new expectations. Carlos and Julie are now deep in conversation. The parade passes: drums, trumpets, Renaissance wigs askew over sheepish grins or faces of unaccustomed solemnity; horses prancing; flags thrown, leapt over, furled and whipped open, as the last swallows dart and glide over the freckled beast pressing down into me.

Whose space am I anyway?

for John M

DESCENDANTS

It's the silence after a knock at the door when my heart jumps a beat. It's when I pick up the letters and speculate on whose hand hit the downstrokes on 'Mrs.', or flowed round the s's in 'Smithson', which office fingers have fluttered over the keys to announce a hidden message inside an envelope addressed to me. Or the blue-grey pause when I lift the receiver, stay a moment and then, 'Joan Smithson speaking' opens another chapter. Usually a disaster.

I couldn't help not being there when Peter died. I had rushed home to fetch clean pyjamas. I feel guilty to this day in spite of what Ian and my friends in the village said at the time. Just that hour or so away, and he had gone, leaving a drift of autumn leaves, our . . . my . . . memories.

Ian said it took me over a year to use 'I' and 'me'. I shuffled among those dry yellow and brown memories, wondering how the things we nagged each other about, even the bickering, bound us as much as our so-called golden hours. It was a shared web of existence, and now silences, pauses, apprehensions were weaving my life. If only he had died when bluebells were carpeting the woods and the skeletons of the trees were still visible, holding the wildest variety of greens, offering the surge of leaf-laden boughs in the breeze and the certainty of summer bouquets. The lambs would have been out by the dry-stone walls in our picture-book Yorkshire village not far from the moors.

Peter had suffered from heart problems for some time. After twenty or more years working in overdrive in the City, men from their late forties onwards usually wear out their hearts. We had discussed plans for years, but it was 'just one more year' to be able to afford our retirement. Then his specialist warned us his heart condition was worsening, so that was it. He just scraped to 60 to get a better pension, and we moved here. It was so tranquil after London. The boys came to help us move in, and I stressed that we had three bedrooms, a bigger house than we needed, so there would be plenty of space for them and their families, when the time came. Ian joked that I was getting 'broody' about being a grandmother. I told him I liked Sarah, his long-standing girlfriend, but he just hugged me and said he wanted to travel and see the world. Then Sarah was replaced by Trish – what a horrible nickname for Patricia! – so I supposed that serial monogamy was the current thing. At least, whoever became his 'partner', as I should say, was always an interesting girl. Sometimes his younger brother, Michael, came along with them.

Michael had lots of ideas about the garden, which was my particular pride and joy. Peter and I enjoyed walking over the moors; that was the main reason we chose Yorkshire. His hobby was building dry-stone walls. I doubted that would be good for his heart, but he insisted the doctors had told him exercise was good, as long as he didn't overdo it. How could a determined person like Peter, who never did anything without an aim and a precise standard to reach, know when he was overdoing things?

I am beginning to upset myself, and that's just what I'm supposed to be getting over by now. Well, we did have a couple of years doing our own things, quite happily settled into our village, when Peter had warning pains and was rushed twenty miles to the nearest hospital. When you retire to a village in the depths of the countryside a hospital isn't exactly round the corner as it is in London. So I had to adjust to living alone when I had been expecting at least ten years of retirement together.

After Peter died everyone in the village dropped in, cooked meals for me, stocked up my larder with the best home-made jams and chutneys. I was welcomed into the Women's Institute, and even helped to start some evening classes. All this did take my mind off things. Of course I knew Peter's health had not been good. It was a shock, but not a shock, if you see what I mean.

I knew what a shock really was when the knock came, but that was about 18 months later.

There was only a difference of 20 months between our boys, and Ian did all the talking for his little brother. We were a bit worried. Michael hardly said more than 'Ma', or 'Dada' until he was three, nearly four. Then he jumped straight into full sentences once his brother left for nursery school. It was odd. Ian was always the taller, the one into sport and girls – far too early in his father's opinion. I let it be. Michael made friends, but they seemed to like quieter things. We sent them to the same school, of course, and, to our surprise, Michael got involved in the drama group. He sort of grew on stage, and I was happy for him. He would beg us to call him 'Mike' as his friends did, but I hated that; it sounded as if someone was always speaking through him. Which I hoped was no longer the case.

Perhaps we shouldn't have sent them to the same school? It's only just occurred to me that it might have been a bad thing. Oh, well, too late now.

Eventually they went their separate ways; Ian – luckily that name could never find some silly abbreviation – always with a gaggle of friends, and girl-friends, I mean partners, one at a time. Peter was a bit worried about letting Ian and the current partner sleep in our spare room as they wanted to, but it had twin beds. Not that it mattered. As Peter said, if they were determined, a mini-car would do. One has to flow with the times . . . and remember one's own youth! Michael? Well, he was different. When he did come to see us, he was always alone. He talked of a few friends he'd like to bring – Pat, Frances or Sam – but he never brought them with him.

That terrible knock came when there was a green haze of new buds on the bare branches. That's why I'm talking to myself because I still can't bear to speak about it to anyone else. I couldn't stop weeping when I heard; then it turned to such deep, violent, silent sobs that Michael made me go to the doctor. He sent me to the bereavement counsellor who said I mustn't push everything that hurts back inside. I had to talk about it, out loud if necessary. To an imaginary person, if no one else was there to listen. Others get bored at the same things over and over again. But it's working, I think. I must stop a moment to try and reflect, and not stuff all those searing moments back deep, deep down inside me.

The knock . . . the kindly policeman, the accident. Then it was just Michael and me.

My friends in the village still dropped in, but they seemed almost frightened to stay. A husband dying is one thing. Age and the passing of years make it a conventional loss. A son's death when still in his twenties is, well, different. I thought at first they were unkind, but in a strange way was also relieved at not having to talk about it. They wouldn't know what to do to staunch the flood of tears, and the sobbing, daylong, nightlong. So they waved at me through the window, in the local corner store, in my garden as I tried to put it to rights. But as I was always weeping or sobbing they kept their distance. I had so much time to think and weep, think and sob. Then it came to me – there was a sort of magic in it all. I had so many gifts, usually placed at my door without knocking. They were offerings at the altar to placate the angry gods, through fear of the unthinkable. That a young person should not live his span. Their children might be the next, but, if the evil eye had fixed its baleful gaze on another, they were somehow saved. The spell was broken – for a while anyway. So they were gifts of relief. Our kindly vicar said I might not be right. He visited me regularly and helped me to talk about Ian's death.

Then there was Michael. He came nearly every weekend. He didn't want to talk about his brother – I could see he was too deeply hurt. We worked together on the garden, went for walks in the bluebell woods; we talked about his work in television. I offered to help sponsor any project he had in mind. My counsellor said that I should develop outside interests, so why not a venture like this? Michael was amazed that I was throwing financial caution to the winds. 'You might lose it all, Mother!' he warned me. We smiled at each other for the first time since Ian's death. I think it was probably the first time I had looked at Michael properly since he was little.

After he'd gone I thought about it, and for the next few days scarcely talked to my imaginary listener, or sobbed. But Michael still puzzled me. He didn't talk about his friends – I thought people in the media were always 'hanging out' in groups. He did occasionally mention Sam, and I reminded him there were two guest rooms. To try and get me to put sound into those chilling silences between us my friends in the village asked if Michael was engaged yet, though they knew that young people don't seem too keen on marriage nowadays. They meant well, but it didn't help because it was what I desperately wanted.

One day the phone rang. I picked it up and the silence between was greyer than ever before 'Joan Smithson'. It was Michael. He asked if he could bring Sam with him that weekend. I was so happy. Perhaps the villagers were right. I started baking.

*   *   *   *   *

I thought Sam would be a girl, knowing how they all shorten names. I have always loathed diminutives. Still, that's what they want to be called. Mike and Sam seem very good friends, and so kind. They kept me company and, really, Sam made such a fuss of me. It reminded me of Peter when we first met, or of Ian in a playful mood. Michael – Mike – just watched, or did back-up jobs like the dishes, or mowing the lawn. I realise they are both young and energetic and only accompanied them up to the brow of the fell beyond the two-acre field, so they could go out into the wilder reaches. That walk was enough for me, and anyway I wanted them to have a good home-baked meal. You know what these young people do nowadays, living on junk food most of the time. Sam is smaller than Michael, chunkier, but fun. Anyway, I'm so glad Michael, I mean Mike, has a friend.

I was so happy after that weekend, and the promise of a longer one with both of them in two weeks' time, that I didn't need any conversations with myself until after I bumped into my counsellor. I hadn't seen her for a few weeks, what with their visit and all the preparations, and somehow my mind was occupied and I wasn't sobbing or anything. Then an overheard remark pitched me into distraught despair. My hearing is too good for my age and own peace of mind. As I went into the local store some days ago I overheard a comment that Joan Smithson's son and his friend walked down the Main Street arm in arm. Mrs. Hallam, the shopkeeper, replied that she was sorry Mrs. Smithson, having lost one son, wouldn't be seeing grandchildren with this one. I left.

I pretended to myself that I had misheard it all, that people wouldn't make such observations. However, as I walked back down Main Street with all those cottage windows and lace curtains, I changed my mind. I decided they were all nasty gossips, shut myself in and didn't move for a week. I didn't open the door when there were callers, nor answer the phone. Letters were left higgledy-piggledy on the door mat, the address a hateful hieroglyphic. I tried to talk it through aloud, but found myself crying differently, a horrid mixture of anger and misery. 'Not me again? Another wallop from fate? Can't I just be left alone to die in my own good time, without more dashing of hopes?' The phone went on ringing, the door-knocker kept crashing down, until I imagined the village gossips imploding on me.

I drew the blinds tight and sat in dull light, though the lilac was blooming as the last of the tulips and forget-me-nots bowed in the summer flowers. Through a small hole in the curtain a ray of sunlight pinpointed a ball of wool that had fallen onto the carpet. It was attached to a pullover I was knitting as a surprise for Michael. I had deliberately set myself the challenge of a difficult cable pattern to please him. Seeing it made me moan as I tried again to unravel the mistake I had made. As I did it, I tried to unpick my feelings, and talked out loud:

Where should I begin? Where the needles are. At the words 'no grandchildren'. That's worth a few tears at the thought of Ian teasing me about being 'broody'. Why did I want them so much? To cuddle them, see them grow up, give them presents. Perhaps I didn't do enough for my boys? I recalled a bachelor friend of Peter's saying that children were a form of self-indulgence, a sort of arrogance and something about one wanting one's genes to fan out in the world, to influence the future. It seemed a lot of rubbish at the time, especially when I thought of all the money we had spent on the two, and all the time, mine especially. I could have had a career, another life. But that's that, and choices have to be made. The bachelor friend droned on – he was one of those who went on and on, probably because he lived alone and grabbed the attention of whoever was there to listen – about Queen Victoria having so many children that she spread haemophilia around the royal families of Europe, and who knows how many unfortunate illegitimates too. Funny I remember this, because I didn't heed it at the time. It must be all about the need to give love, and the cold blue-grey silence of the tomorrows without the babble of children.

The sobs are returning, and tears are welling up. Oh dear, I can't stop remembering that deep joy in the comforting sound Ian made when he was happily absorbed in some hobby in his room. He always left the door open to keep the flow of contact, but used to hum or even say a phrase or two to himself. It was before the days when they all got their hi-fis and couldn't bear their own quiet.

I'm thinking things I couldn't say to anyone, not even to Peter, no one. It's a relief to be able to get it out of me without any repercussions. With others there's always a reckoning, but not with an imaginary friend. It may seem that I've lived a relatively sheltered life, but I have always been interested in what's going on around me. One does need to keep up with the world one's children are living in. Anyway, Peter and I always considered ourselves enlightened liberals, supportive of minority groups. I slightly regretted not having a daughter, you know, because I would have made sure she had more opportunities than I did. Funny, that women's rights should be lumped in with 'minority rights' when I think we are a majority. Anyway, it's the right to live one's own life without harming others that Peter and I always supported, if rather passively.

Why shouldn't two men – or women also, I suppose – live together if they want to? That is their choice, over a certain age, of course. There were two older men who frequented a pub I often went to with Peter. They sat in the window seat holding hands, and no-one paid any attention. We thought we were so tolerant. But nearer home. Well, it never occurred to either of us that we could have a son who . . . Oh yes, I know now how easy it is to be tolerant in theory. At a distance. But when it's right there in front of you, and there's no one to confide in, then – it doesn't make me angry, only sad and diminished as a woman.

Now why should I feel like that? I can only say this into thin air, but it seems to be a rejection of me, of my innermost self, of what makes me 'me'. Now I have to go into what gives me an identity. What am I, deep down? First a person – or a woman? Or first a woman, female, my gender, then a person? I suspect, at least in my present state of mind, the former. So if my son rejects women, then it hurts me too. Is this muddled thinking? Then there's the mother aspect. For us it's easier, I suppose, if you think about it. We are born from another like us, but men, in the act of love, return to where they came from. It might be subconsciously terrifying. I wouldn't know, but I'm sure it has been theorised to extinction in numerous books on psychology.

I am even more knotted inside because Michael is the son who resembles me. Ian was all Peter, with a few extra inches on top. I've unravelled the wool and am ready to tackle the complicated cable bit again, but I'm too confused to go on now. Peter would say, 'A cup of tea, Joan, is what you need.' I'm sad, puzzled, but not despairing. It helps to talk like this, turn it over in one's mind as if someone were really . . . '

* * * * *

I haven't been pondering for days because before I could make that cup of tea there was a thunderous knocking, followed by someone shouting, 'Mrs. Smithson, please open. We're the police!' I thought they were trying to break down the door. What a commotion! They said my son had been phoning and phoning me without getting an answer, and had finally called them in. I could hardly pull the door open for the clutter of post and newspapers. Outside were remains of packages of food that cats had been banqueting on, milk bottles, the lot. I phoned Michael immediately, at work.

Before he arrived the next evening I tried to tidy up a bit. It was a mess. I wasn't sure I could deal with the post, but I did sort the hand-written ones. There were three from Michael, and a nice one from Sam thanking me for the weekend and saying he hoped he could return. I put them under the lamp, next to the pullover, and decided to try and eat something.

They had taken the first train after lunch and hired a car in York. I wasn't allowed to cook a meal. We went to a country pub some miles away and had venison, just as Peter and I did, for a special occasion. Saturday dawned sunny. Michael and Sam invited me to go for a walk with them, but I said my ankle was playing up, which wasn't true. I felt too fragile to face the villagers. The young men had something up their sleeves when they returned, as they drove off to our market town to do some shopping. Mike told me they were cooking the meal. This was serious culinary business, it seemed. They came back quite early and bumped into, of all people, Mrs. Hallam from our local shop, who had popped in with a few things she thought I might need. As a gift. She said she'd been worried, 'Not seeing me, and all that,' adding that she thought my son's friend 'looked a nice, sensible sort of young man'.

Sam busied himself in the kitchen with the bags and bottles. Michael suggested we all had a drink. He took one out to Sam and returned, closing the kitchen door behind him.

'I was so worried, Mother. I phoned and phoned and imagined the unimaginable. Sorry about calling the police. What happened?'

'I don't know. Something snapped inside me. I didn't want to eat anything, hear anything, see anyone. For once I wanted the silence, the deepest blue-grey possible. So I drew the curtains.'

'But why? I thought you enjoyed that weekend. We did.'

'So did I, but . . . '

'I think we ought to talk. Don't you? Without making impossible claims, emotionally or in any other way . . . '

'That's all very well, Michael, but I can't stop feeling, being hurt. And worse, not being able to find a reason for it all. I didn't want to tell you, but they started talking down in the village. "Poor Mrs. Smithson", that sort of thing.'

'Mother, they're kind people, and are obviously upset for you about Ian. You've had a tough time. Two bereavements in 20 months. It's hit me too. A lot.'

'No. Worse. They were gossiping about you, all I have left. You.'

'Me?'

'I didn't want to tell you. Let's forget it and talk of something else. No. That's just what my counsellor told me not to do. Let's talk about it.'

'I can't believe it. About me? What have I done to merit comment?'

'Holding hands with Sam.'

'Mother, didn't you know?'

'Why should I? You never said anything. All I wanted was for you to be happy in the way of life you had chosen. I didn't feel it was for me to pry. Since father died, it's been a struggle to cope here, alone.'

'I did try to help.'

'You did.'

'What did they say?'

'Just a chance remark in the shop, that Joan Smithson wouldn't have any grandchildren.'

'Well, some gay couples do, but we weren't thinking of that. Try to see life in a more open-ended way. Allow yourself some hope.'

'I thought I was tolerant. I hope I still am. Perhaps I wasn't a good mother, but I did try to do my best . . . '

'It's nothing to do with you, mother. It's probably not what I might have chosen, had there been a choice. Having Ian ahead of me made me realise his way wasn't mine. But that's a long story, and he was a good brother to me. Just very different. I too have a right . . . '

'I know you do. But so do I. Can't I be honest with you? I believe that being "straight" or whatever one should say, is the happiest way of things. It's sort of accepting the excitement and mystery of the other person, different, reciprocal. At least, in the best of relations. I had that with Peter, and wanted it, naturally, for my children. I can't change what I think – but I don't expect you to agree. As we all wish the best for our children, so I wished it for you and Ian. Having said that, it's my view, and I don't force it on you or anyone else.'

'Mrs. Smithson, Mike, the meal's ready!'

'Do call me Joan. You know, I've long thought it presumptuous that women for nearly a century now have commandeered male clothes, trousers, waistcoats, even ties. Why shouldn't men – don't laugh – do the same?'

'We might make a start with kilts!'

❧❧

for Hideo and Nabuko, and Reiko

❧❧

HAPPY BIRTHDAY, CHARLOTTE!

It was at my 'crammer' school that I encountered Charlotte. I was sent to this school at eight, the same age when she was sent away from home; her mother had died two years earlier. My parents 'died' under the funereal shadow of Uncle Hiroshi, my mother's elder brother. He used his brilliant business skills to control my parents. In the guise of helping his sister, he dominated us three children, having none of his own. He informed us we would not inherit any of his considerable fortune unless we behaved perfectly. We were left in no doubt, my brother and I, that when we were enrolled in the best crammer in Tokyo at considerable cost to him, excellence was the only possible outcome: excellence in learning, excellence in behaviour, and excellence in our future careers. Destiny weighed heavily upon us.

It is a commonplace to say that languages learnt early are learnt well, but without reading Charlotte Brontë my passion for the English language might not have expanded beyond the bounds of everyday necessity. Our teacher was in her personality unmemorable, but her instruction was thorough and varied, threaded with a carefully controlled passion for English literature early revealed in her choice of English songs to sing to us, moving on to ballads of lost loves, poems of flower-scattered meadows and woods alive with birdsong. When we left ballads for stories, she ordered us to buy an English reader with extracts from great novels so thick that the binding loosened the pages. As if intended, it would fall open at the middle revealing the following passage:

'How dare you affirm that, Jane Eyre?'
'How dare I, Mrs. Reed? How dare I? Because it is the truth. You think I have no feelings, and that I can do without one bit of love or kindness; but I cannot live so: and you have no pity. I shall remember how you thrust me back – roughly and violently thrust me back – into the red-room, and locked me up there, to my dying day; though I was in agony; though

I cried out, while suffocating with distress, "Have mercy! Have mercy, Aunt Reed!" And that punishment you made me suffer because your wicked boy struck me – knocked me down for nothing. I will tell anybody who asks me questions, this exact tale. People think you a good woman, but you are bad, hardhearted. *You* are deceitful!'

Ere I had finished this reply, my soul began to expand, to exult, with the strangest sense of freedom, of triumph, I ever felt. It seemed as if an invisible bond had burst, and that I had struggled out into unhoped-for liberty.'

Our teacher explained the vocabulary first, exploring gently the meaning of the words, pointing to the use of tenses to remind us of a grammatical rule lurking in the recesses of our minds. As she expounded, pink spots appeared on each cheek. Her agitation seemed more difficult to control when she discussed the meaning of the whole passage, of Aunt Reed's cruelty in those far-off days; distant though those times were, I sensed that Charlotte Brontë spoke in a way easier to feel than to understand. Every time I started my English homework, the reader fell open at the same page. I read the passage over and over and noted again with surprise the powerful feelings, so unusual for someone to express at the time, since the heroine was addressing the very one who was providing for her; all this both intrigued and troubled my mind.

I am speaking of nearly 15 years ago, but all that I tell you is as fresh in my mind as if it happened yesterday, when I toiled over my homework in the room I shared with my brother on the top floor of Uncle Hiroshi's house. Space in Japan is strictly rationed, never more so than in the environs of Tokyo. Uncle Hiroshi, with his customary foresight, had taken all the money he and his sister had inherited from their father, and had bought a plot in the countryside near Tokyo where a new metropolitan underground line was planned. It was indeed a sound financial investment. As was his wont, Uncle Hiroshi never stopped reminding us of his foresight; it hung over us like a thundercloud, ready to burst upon any unsuspecting member of our family who did not show himself suitably grateful. Such pronouncements were rarely addressed to the women in the family: my Aunt Sayoko barely figured except at the meals she had prepared, for the kitchen was her domain. Having shown herself incapable of child-bearing, there was nothing else for her to do.

Thus released from the cares and consolations of the domestic scene, and with all children able to walk, our mother was directed to whatever occupation she could find within reasonable distance of the family house which allowed her to be present when her children returned from school. All good positions, however, were only to be found in the centre of Tokyo which was an hour's journey by train, so Mother had little choice of work in our district which, being rapidly built up, provided principally employment in the construction area. Trained as a teacher, she had to accept a position of secretary in a local school. Frequently admonished by Uncle Hiroshi to look after her children, Mother was at a loss to know what exactly was meant by this since we could wash and feed ourselves. Consequently she wore a careworn look like a frayed apron, as she alternated between peering into our bedroom door where we were studying to see if we needed anything (I cannot believe my uncle required her to spy on us to see if his investment in our education was likely to reap adequate returns), or wandering into the kitchen to help Aunt Sayoko, who would set her to the most menial tasks of washing up, chopping or scrubbing utensils.

Father, on the other hand, after applying for various positions in the engineering field and failing to penetrate the employment structure of emerging international firms, ended up in a junior position in Uncle Hiroshi's business. It was not his choice, yet he bore it with fortitude, punctilious to a degree, always returning home later than his brother-in-law. For my poor father, an unpleasant and somewhat ingratiating duty this turned out to be. Uncle Hiroshi, mercurial by nature, would return home early, soon after nine, or on another occasion after midnight, having succumbed to one of the numerous temptations our capital city discreetly offers to businessmen after hours. It was some years before I understood why the telephone rang and rang after nine o'clock with Mother rushing to answer it to let Father know if he should return. Meanwhile my elder brother would groan at this disturbance while he was dutifully absorbed in his studies.

My elder brother regarded me from a distance as if we were worlds apart, though sharing the same not very large bedroom; he saw me as if from the wrong end of binoculars, a view justified by his three years of seniority. My sister was different in every way; though two years older, she was my greatest companion. One day – I recall it vividly – Mother and Father unexpectedly and uncharacteristically decided that, as my brother had gained a school prize, they would take him and our sister to the top of the Shinjuku Centre Building, at that time the highest building in Tokyo. It was a great treat because one could see so far, enjoy the delights of games and food in many restaurants, and be just where everyone else aspired to go. Unknown to my parents, it was a place that young rebellious teenagers were beginning to frequent, sometimes even with a girlfriend. I was excluded from this excursion; I had too much to prepare for important examinations. Furious, frustrated, but too frightened to protest, I retired to our bedroom with a book. While the rest of the family enjoyed this rare treat, I would not study but spent the time with Charlotte. At 13 I could read the full and unabridged text of *Jane Eyre* and was now regarded as incomparably the best student of English in the whole crammer.

When I was young I accepted without question that my sister would go to the local school and not join us at the expensive crammer in Tokyo. As I grew older my sister's situation concerned me more. Then one day, when I was about 12, I asked my parents who informed me that it was Uncle Hiroshi's decision to economise by using local schools for her. So she never knew my English teacher, learnt no English until she was old enough to go to the local High School. But I told her all about Charlotte Brontë and *Jane Eyre*, and for her birthday each year I would give her translations of the English books I was reading, so we could talk and imagine that faraway land together. Our chosen world of literature became the secret land we inhabited together. Then one morning, a terrible event occurred. Five years after she started at the High School, my sister fell from the platform onto the rails in front of the local train she was waiting for, and was killed.

'The way your daughter has died is the way people commit suicide in our country,' stormed Uncle Hiroshi, incensed at the shame he would have to suffer as head of the family.

'Suicide?' whispered Father. 'They said she was joking with other girls waiting together at the same designated spot where the train stops and the doors open. Someone must have pushed her in jest.'

'Nonsense!' roared Uncle Hiroshi, leaving my father to make the customary public apology, ending with his declared intention of paying all the expenses incurred. Mother wiped tears away when she thought no one was looking; while my brother remained grim-faced and stoical, I hid as far as possible from everyone in my secret hiding-place under the stairs. There in the company of brushes, dust pans and a vacuum cleaner, I found comfort in reading. There after my sister's death I began speaking in my mind to Charlotte.

One day soon after the accident a shrine appeared in the area off the kitchen where we used to eat. It was a small square box set on a low table; I could see it as I sat opposite, cross-legged on a mat during our meals. Uncle Hiroshi objected to its presence; it reminded him of the family shame and the resulting damage to his professional and social status, It would have to be removed. My sister's shrine disappeared upstairs to our parents' room; I visited her there, praying towards the red light like dying embers where her spirit was cherished; Mother often stayed there with me and being together offered us mute consolation. Father chose to bicycle out beyond the building sites into what remained of the countryside before the cultivated land ended and the rocky terrain rising to the mountains began; whatever time he could find away from his family obligations was spent painting birds and waterfalls, willow trees and mountains.

Oh, Charlotte, I longed for your wilder landscape,
'Like heath that, in the wilderness
the wild wind whirls away.'

I too
'Wished the wind to howl more wildly, the gloom to deepen
to darkness, and the confusion to rise to clamour.'

I felt the wind across the heath; I saw the bleak cold whiteness of winter bursting into spring with a profusion of snowdrops, crocuses, daffodils and bluebells in the woods where new leaves scattered shade and light and quiet contentment. I imagined birds nesting, a glimpse of a hare, sly foxes; all nature alert. Rainstorms, then sunshine and hope. I was to find some kind of peace as my education proceeded along the dutiful path set by Uncle Hiroshi – school, exams, success; university, exams, success – all the time my comfort, and my deepest feelings found their expression in writing letters to Charlotte, my mentor and companion in my loneliness. I never posted them, afraid a real person at the Haworth Parsonage might find and read them: they were for you, Charlotte, you alone. Your birthday is on 21 April, just when spring brings a breath of hope, but within all its beauty you told of typhoid and death at Lowood School where Jane Eye's friend, Helen Burns, died; so like my sister, she did not rebel, just accepted and believed; she understood all you and I feel. Instead of words I send you flowers with my thoughts, the colours of sun, of leaf and sky; rays of hope and scents of things to come.

The year I bought my last school diary I drew a snowdrop on the page for 21 April, and then wondered whether April was late for snowdrops in England. In my first college diary I added a daffodil; by the time I had my first position as a junior engineer in 'one of Japan's foremost companies', I could not resist adding a bluebell on 21 April in my company diary. I decided that year not just to draw the flowers but to send them. No name, no address, just 'Happy birthday, Charlotte!' So now I could imagine the bouquet arriving at the Parsonage in Haworth, hoping it was not placed on her gravestone. I imagined my spring flowers on a windowsill, framed by the stone surround of a small aperture onto the moors, just turning green and blue in the distance and the first lambs in the nearby meadows. There I could imagine Charlotte; she became my ally, my friend, when I was alone in my sister's room, writing tedious reports, or bending over numbers, theorems, engineering theory and practice – so many hours spent as a cog in the wheel of factory work. But I never forgot 21 April and your bouquet.

It was not long after I began celebrating your birthday that Uncle Hiroshi, economising as usual, decided that my brother and I should be introduced to some marriageable young ladies of a suitable class, background, and, above all, purity. The Japanese do not desire any marriage partner to bear even the slightest trace of the primitive inhabitants of this country. Some families, when a marriage is intended, employ detective agencies to look into the forebears of a bride or groom, not just their family's wealth. I was too young and too immersed in my dreams to be at all interested, but my brother had begun to show regard for women, and that Uncle Hiroshi saw as a warning sign that SOMETHING MUST BE DONE, AND SOON. At 19 my brother had started university where he might, Uncle Hiroshi declared, associate with unsuitable company. From then onwards there were perpetual introductions to daughters of his colleagues and acquaintances. All were sweetly subdued, pretty and well groomed; all lacked passion and personality. I at least was unmoved: I would make my own choice, Uncle Hiroshi or not. He preached about people in the West who fell in love and married whoever they fancied, ignoring their parents' wishes. All inevitably ended in divorce and family misery. Not so in our country, Uncle Hiroshi proclaimed: arranged marriages were the only way to ensure happiness because parents knew what was best for their children. These marriages had to work, and so they did. When Uncle Hiroshi was in the mood to speak thus, my mind would wander to the passage in *Jane Eyre* placed right in the middle of the book where it always fell open, and I remembered my English teacher – I could never forget the pink spots in her cheeks. Not just women, Charlotte '. . . need exercise for their faculties, and a field for their efforts . . . suffer from too rigid a restraint, too absolute a stagnation'.

By the time I was nearly 30, some daughters of rich industrialists were, Uncle Hiroshi said, seeking me as a husband. I had moved to start work in his firm: there my brother had predictably inherited Uncle Hiroshi's position, though in retirement he still pulled strings. They were all, Charlotte, attractive; that is, all well dressed and behaved, reserved, assiduous, everything except interesting. They still had fans, still giggled behind them, still said what was expected: in short, they seemed to have been educated to obedience like Aunt Sayoko and Mother. But Jane rebelled.

'You think I have no feelings . . . Ere I had finished this reply, my soul began to expand, to exult, with the strangest sense of freedom, of triumph, I ever felt. It seemed as if an invisible bond had burst, and that I had struggled out into unhoped-for liberty.'

These young ladies wouldn't understand. My sister did. It's early April, Charlotte, time to send you your birthday flowers.

At last in late April this year I found time to go to the Shinjuku Centre Building; you could not imagine how long I had thought of going since that time so many years ago I was made to stay at home and study. After my sister died it became a place to avoid; now it was time to overcome that reluctance. I went many times in April, a month of unfolding, of the flowers I imagine framed in the stone casement window of the Parsonage at Haworth: your flowers, Charlotte. White, yellow, blue on a green leaf background, they danced in my mind as I entered the Shinjuku Centre Building, stepping lightly through the halls to the lift, then up in excitement to the top where the city lay at my feet, the vastness of the metropolis as it spread infinitely seawards on one side, to the mountains on the other. I sensed something romantic might happen. Couples were huddled deep in conversation on the seats. On my fourth visit I noticed a girl sitting apart, gazing at the view, and holding a book which she opened, then closed to look out and dream. She stood up and walked across to the windows, leaving her book on the seat. I glanced at the cover. It was *Jane Eyre*. Charlotte, I plucked up courage, began to speak to her, and thus I fell in love with one who possesses 'a beauty neither of fine colour nor of long eyelash, nor pencilled brow, but of meaning, of movement, of radiance'. This was my quest rewarded, my romantic dream, my freedom to choose a person to love.

Predictably, Uncle Hiroshi refused to consider Yuka a suitable bride for me because her family was not sufficiently well-placed. He protested unsuitability, threatened to have me dismissed from his firm, disinherited. So, to the horror of my parents and my brother's disgust, I confronted Uncle Hiroshi.

'Do you think because you have kept my parents and their children poor, obscure and beholden to you, that I have no personality and sentiment? You think wrong! If God had gifted me with power and wealth, I should have made it impossible for you to dominate me and my family. I am not talking to you now through the medium of custom, conventionalities or tradition, but of my freedom to choose. I shall marry the person I know I love, not your choice nor anyone else's.'

Happy birthday, Charlotte!

Oh, I nearly forgot, my e-mail is makoto@xjyft.ne.jp.

Yorkshire moorland

ಹಿ‌ಿ

for Alexandra, Lynn and Michael

ಲ‌ಿ

THE SCARF

It was precious from the start, even the paper wrapping it. Maggie saved everything: scraps of wrapping paper, bits of string, used envelopes that still had flap and glue intact. Every Christmas she had to run the gauntlet of family teasing as she carefully retrieved, patted out the creases and stored away the paper for the following year, just as her mother had done before her. This paper was embossed, with a dancingly handsome design in red and gold, reminiscent of rippling water and of gondolas.

It had been a happy tour from the outset. No anonymous letter pinned onto the plush side of the lift, no tantrums because a room was too claustrophobic, the shower too small, no bath, no view, too noisy. Strange with a group of 28 where the law of averages decrees that there should be two and five-eighths problems precisely! From the start they had spun a web of alert enthusiasm. Maggie was overjoyed.

So here she was at the drinks before the farewell dinner, about to desecrate that alluring wrapping paper to reveal the contents. Her hands trembled, more at the embarrassment of what she could say in thanks than in anticipation of what it contained. Nobody would ever believe that she, who lectured unabashed in an auditorium filled with hundreds of people, had a stomach that shrank to the size of a pea at a personal speech of thanks. Clearly it wasn't the usual book that someone would be delegated to find out whether it was what she had secretly longed for but couldn't afford. The package was too small and soft for that, her apprehension the greater. Well, eyes were on her, everyone was silent in expectation. She now had to stand up and do her bit. She pumped up the adrenaline and eased open the paper, trying as far as possible to keep it intact.

There it lay before her, a scarf echoing the colours of the wrapping paper but with variations too miraculous to imagine. It was a cashmere design with a difference; it told of the centuries-old deep gold and crimson of icons, of the shell-shaped hollows of dark blue and creamy white in the ripples on the canals, of the deeply-etched profiles of the alleys and the swaying arabesque shadows cast by the lanterns, of the tingle of exotic spices, the laughter in hidden courtyards, the scent of summer jasmine, and of intimacy.

'It's the best we could find.' Linda broke the silence.

'Pure silk, hand made, very Venetian we thought,' Amy added.

'We looked for something that would suit you, but wasn't blue. You already have a blue Indian scarf, so this had to be different.' Liz was aware of Maggie's embarrassment, and tried to feed her some cues. 'How d'you feel about it?'

Did she like it? It was beyond her wildest imaginings! She could see it was the finest silk without even handling it, which she was fearful of doing in case an unfiled nail or rough skin would catch it, a fate too unbearable even to contemplate. She hesitated, almost in tears, before uttering the usual platitudes.

'So generous . . . can't thank you enough . . . such a kind thought . . . just what I wanted . . . you have been a wonderful group . . .' All true, but so excruciatingly predictable.

'Don't forget the gondola trip after dinner, Maggie,' Linda reminded her. 'And please wear the scarf.'

Richard had been watching from a table near the back, somewhat amused. He swept by her on the way out with a whisper, 'It's very costly. I know. I've bought another similar one. I'm thinking of wrapping it round the flex on my chandelier in the sitting-room at home.'

Imagine an embracingly warm June evening when the last suspicion of the rosy sunset let loose a scatter of bats over the gondolas. Maggie felt apprehensive about wearing the scarf. It was too valuable to be worn in a gondola. She should dart back to her room and put it in a safe place. It was warm enough not to need it, but she'd been asked to wear it, giving her an unaccustomed swagger as she left the hotel with the gondola group. 'A touch of class,' she murmured to herself, immediately eating her words. She didn't need any sort of boost; she was who she was, no more no less. A garment couldn't change that. In any case, she wore her disgust at the regimentation of fashion on her very well displayed metaphorical sleeve for all to see. She was too much of an individual to follow mass dictates. But those of people she admired, that's another matter. She arranged the silken shawl with delicate pleasure round her neck, ready for whatever that night held in store.

This vision of silent backwaters with their velvet shadowy silences, punctuated by bursts of light, a babble of voices, a child's cry or the hushed whispers of lovers – so timeworn, so acclaimed in every language of the world from the dawn of travel – rose phoenix-like anew. The 'I've seen it all' of the most jaded traveller was soothed away; they were all phoenixes now in a city where buildings peeled, sank lop-sided cheek by jowl with their scaffolding-clad neighbours busily being repointed or replastered. Venice decaying: Venice arising.

Gliding into the main thoroughfare, the glitz of packaged, processed delights broke the spell. Groaning gondolas, five abreast, their inhabitants champagne-swigging, strawberry-scoffing to the trite delights of *Funicoli, funicola*, ding a dong a dinga dong a dingi do dee da ... an incongruous Neapolitan ditty more appropriate to the ascent of Vesuvius by mechanical means. 'Spare me that indignity!' Maggie thought, wondering why the muse of the first vacation city in the post-Roman world couldn't at least produce some suitable ditty for operatic gondoliers to enhance their hire value. Offered the wide waters of the Grand Canal, the full moon skittishly scattered her silver dowry out past the Custom House capped by the glowing gilded dome, carved the water by the still growling lion of St. Mark and strewed yet more coins far out into the lagoon, just missing the floodlit mass of San Giorgio Maggiore by a metre or a mile, no matter.

'*Luna piena, acqua alta,*' boomed their *gondolier*, who fortunately didn't sing. Sent by the Adriatic beyond the barrier island, a breeze coyly tugged at the scarf that slid its silken sheen over Maggie's shoulder.

'I'll lose it! I should never have come out on a gondola with it. Why don't I take care of the lovely things I'm given!' And then, in growing anxiety, 'Should I tie a knot?' An eddy of air, a sharp turn of her shoulder to catch sight of a group playing lutes on a balcony of lacy Istrian stone, a – her tense hand grasped the two ends like an incongruous makeshift brooch, and the gondola glided on and round and back.

When she held out the other hand for her room key in the haven of the hotel – she thought they were eyeing her scarf from the reception desk, estimating it with Venetian shrewdness – they reminded her, '*Luna piena, acqua alta, professoressa.*'

'You mean the Piazza di San Marco is under water?'

'Of course. And rising too.'

No time to lose. Maggie turns half-running till she senses the gleam and dampening of sound in the Piazza from a passage leading to the portico. She abandons her sandals on the plinth of a column and wades out into the warm water to join cigarette butts, Fanta cans and pigeon droppings to reach a knot of intrepids gesticulating at her. Linda, Amy, Liz and a host of others, beckon her into their version of a dance to Diana, goddess of the moon, while Richard and his stag party cheer from the sidelines, retreating back under the portico as the lapping monster devours one more step and attacks another.

Disaster or occasional disturbance, whatever, the musicians at Florian's retreat and play on, the strings dropping a tone or two in deference to the rising humidity. 'That's the Venetian version of a stiff upper lip,' Maggie applauds, as she strides out towards the floodlit Basilica, anchored at the far end, casting its glittering mosaics into jewelled splinters where children splash to catch them, aped by spellbound adults. Maggie begins to dance and sing and, as the shawl slips, she pulls it with her right hand and swirls it round her head.

Even the sages atop the library of St. Mark are looking down approvingly at the spirits unleashed by Diana, the huntress. Intrepid souls are out prowling the waters between the empty palace, the Doge consigned safely to history, and the rim of the lagoon usually pegged out by expectant gondolas. No longer. They have lost their moorings; the red and white poles are discreetly swooning below water.

'Guess where the poles are,' Maggie dares herself. To her right the dome of the Customs House is gathering moonlight in homage, and Palladio's masterpiece, San Giorgio Maggiore, is floating towards her across the dark waters fretted with moonlight. Families with small children a-piggy-back, squealing with delight; youths splashing in sport, heaving away to renew the feigned attack, legs ever more leaden in the rising waters; a slow motion rock and roll starts up between two columns behind her. St. Theodore and St. Mark's lion look down from them in amazement, though they have seen worse. Diana the huntress is scattering moonbeams alongside San Giorgio.

'Catch a moonbeam!' Maggie shouts, and strides on towards the church, which seems close enough. On, on and then the piazza relinquishes space to the lagoon.

The deep water dashes her into consciousness. Head surfaces, eyes open to see the scarf spread out like an isosceles triangle, apex towards the moon and another angle pointing at San Giorgio. She lunges at it without any ground to give impetus, and falls flat onto the water. Head bobbing up again and every moon-rimmed ripple seems to be the elusive scarf. 'Got you!' and Maggie strikes out towards the moon, grabbing at dark patches to trawl empty cans and cigarette packets, a wilting newspaper, a tourist's map – debris of tourist consumption. 'Where is that fabric of adventure, that silk from the Barbary coast?'

Maggie intones to Diana, turning her strokes towards Palladio's monumental temple facade, which retreats at each lunge. Then tired, defeated, cold and no longer exhilarated, she turns tail to regain the Piazzetta, stubbing her foot on one of those barber-like gondola mooring poles to fall headlong into the warm shallows, missing a cigarette butt or pigeon excrement by a hairsbreadth.

What can she say? Priceless gift lost. It's the moon's fault. She should have put it back carefully in the white tissue and embossed wrapping paper, to be cherished at home on special occasions, for the weddings, anniversaries of the shadowy future. She can still feel the fabulously soft caress of the silk, the fine magician's weave of red, right royal purple, and the deepest blue you can imagine, a suspicion of moss green swooning into gold, and then a saturated velvet green of indescribable glory, an Aladdin's cave, a tissue of jokes, accounts, queries, teasing, confided hopes and fears and the fun of the last three weeks, of the Lindas, Amys, Lizes and the others, even Richard.

But his will be wound safely round the flex. Hers, washed up on the shore of San Giorgio, is still a warm, invisible web woven around her memory.

Doge's Palace, towards San Giorgio